Roxy May

Help my Granda is Haunting me!

Nicola Ormerod

Published by Karabeth Publishing

Edited by Emma Hawkins

Cover Design by

David Porter

Model
Dara More

ISBN
978-1-908505-86-6

For my Mum, an angel

Although the characters in this book are completely fictional there is one exception. Roxanne May's grandfather Finlay McDonald is based on my Granda also named Finlay McDonald. He sadly passed away a few years ago now and I miss him dearly. Writing this book has really helped me cope with the grief of losing him. He was a wonderful strong man, gentle at the same time and so full of love.

I would also like to thank my dear mother. She passed away two years ago and it's been really hard coming to terms with it. Only good friends and a wonderful husband have been able to get me through it. She never got to read any of my work but I know she was so proud of everything I did. I miss you mum.

She was, on more than one occasion placed in the Lancashire Hospice for rest and respice and £1.00 from every paperback sold will be donated in her memory.

The nurses and staff are truelly wonderful there and I know it was a place of peace for my mum.

To my husband Simon, who works extra hard to enable me to follow my dream and passion to write instead of getting a proper job. He's a wonderful man and my soulmate in every way.

I want to also say thank you to Simon's family who have supported us and been there in the darkest of times, thank you. My mother in law Linda, who upon the passing of my own mother has taken me under her wing. Every girl needs a mummy.

And last but by no means least to Emma Hawkins, my new friend, I am honoured that you took the time to edit this book, you have done a wonderful job.

Roxy May

Help my Granda is Haunting me!

Chapter 1

"Mum, where's my new hair band?"

"It's in the bathroom honey."

"No not the pink one, the black one."

"No idea Rox and if you don't hurry up you're going to be late."

I muttered under my breath and began looking through my dressing table drawers. It was the first day of my fourth year at secondary school. I was excited and scared at the same time. Excited because I'd be seeing more of my crush Brandon (more on him in a minute) and scared because school is a 'dog eat dog' place, or should I say 'cow eat cow' because we have a fair few in our year.

It's hard to believe that day was only a couple of months ago. Harder still to believe are the things that I know now and the things I was totally ignorant of back then. The transition from being a normal teenager, whose main problems were getting homework done on time and a spot appearing on my face, to a teenager who was thrust into a supernatural world was fast, really fast. Would I go back and be the old me if I could? Nope, definitely not. The world is a magical place full of creatures you wouldn't believe.

1

Help my Granda is Haunting Me!

My name is Roxanne May McDonald but my friends and family call me Roxy or Rox. I live in Aberdeen with my mum and I'm an only child. My mum brought me up single-handedly because my dad left before I was even born; he didn't even know my mum was pregnant. She, along with the help of my grandparents raised me and they've done a pretty good job I think. Our family is small but extremely close knit and I like that; my grandparents were as big a factor in my life as my mum was. I go to a private school here too and I'm not blowing my own trumpet, well I suppose I am, but I'm quite clever. I get straight A's and I actually like my school work, especially maths. I could probably be a little more popular if I wasn't so clever but I have the sense not to dumb down for a few extra popularity points.

But going back to that first day; I stared at myself in my dressing table mirror, reached for my straighteners and gave my hair a last quick going over. I then made a point of unplugging them because mum said she was going to chuck them in the bin if I left them switched on once more.

I'd had my long brown hair cut the previous week and I now had an up to date super side fringe. Unfortunately it hated being a side fringe and needed holding in place with a can of hairspray; no pain without gain though. I kept the length because I liked it, the downside being if I wanted it to look nice and straight I needed at least half an hour to forty minutes. I am blessed with brains but I am not blessed with naturally straight hair.

2

Our school uniform is horribly old-fashioned with a green and yellow blazer. Mum won't let me have an above the knee skirt either so I look like a nerd the minute I step out the door. This year mum relented and bought me some really nice black flat ballerina type slipper/shoes and my fabulous nana bought me a really trendy shoulder bag from Debenhams. My mum had suggested a rucksack and I admit I sulked (I'm fifteen!), until nana relented and bought it for me. I was instantly happy until later in the confines of my bedroom I discovered that I couldn't fit a folder into it. I was keeping my lips sealed in case mum took it back.

The front door buzzer rang out. I pressed the button on the intercom to release the lock on the outside door at the bottom of the stairs so my two best friends could come upstairs to our flat. If you've never visited Aberdeen then I'll tell you this; the city centre, and about a mile radius surrounding it, is mostly flats. We have heaps of sky scrapers and then your more traditional granite flats, which is what we lived in.

My mum poked her head out of the kitchen.

"I have toast here."

"It's OK mum I'm not hungry."

"Take it, I swear Roxanne if you can't get more organised you'll have to get up earlier."

"It's the hair, took ages to straighten," I said as I let my two friends in.

"Yes and there's a cloud of hairspray following you around too, oh hi Jennifer, Annabel. You girls ready for the first day back?"

"Yes Mrs McDonald," they answered together.

"Right mum, we've got to go."

I grabbed the toast, stuffed my folder under my arm (stupid trendy bag!) and we headed out onto the street. We all stayed pretty close to our school on Queen Street near the main road in Aberdeen and our morning ritual usually consisted of us stopping at Starbucks, if we had time, for a hot chocolate to start the day. We were cutting it fine with my lateness but Starbucks do THE best hot chocolate so it was worth the risk.

"Guess who I saw yesterday in Union Square?"Annabel asked us excitedly.

Annabel was one of my best friends. She was this tiny thing with blonde hair and she was really pretty. She sometimes got a hard time because her parents were really poor and they could never afford to buy her expensive clothes. Like me, her grandparents paid for her education but her mum struggled to manage money properly. Annabel had hinted that her parents were in a lot of debt. Being at a private school is fifty times harder than regular school because of the pressure to have the best and most expensive stuff. Generally I'm happy with New Look and high street shops; you can still look nice and not spend two hundred pounds on a belt.

4

A lot of Annabel's clothes were bought from charity shops and she shopped for most of it herself. Stuff like that has never mattered a jot to me and it annoyed the hell out of me when some of the other girls would take the mick out of her.

Jennifer was my other best friend. She was gorgeous and always dressed impeccably but she was really down to earth. Although her parents were wealthy she fitted in with our little trio perfect. My two best gals; I adored them.

Jennifer and I waited impatiently for Annabel's response.

"Brandon!"

"No way," I gushed. "I have been dying to see him all summer."

"He was with his mum, she is way pretty and so sophistamacated."

"Lucky cow," pouted Jennifer.

Brandon was, and still is, the best looking boy I have ever set eyes on and I totally fancied the pants off him. I had known him since we started school over three years ago and in that time he had gone from a cute boy to a six foot tall young man. Whenever I saw him my knees lost the power to function properly. He had dark chocolate brown hair which he wore in a shaggy cut like Edward from *Twilight* but he was way nicer to look at and way more mysterious. He had pale blue eyes and, thanks to swimming and playing rugby for the school, he was well-built too. I sighed just thinking about him.

"I don't know why we bother fancying him," I said to my friends. "I mean we don't stand a chance of ever bagging him, it's wasted energy."

"I know but he is uber-lovely," Jennifer replied.

"Totally," agreed Annabel. "And he is so nice, it's not like he blanks us."

It was true. In all the years I had known him he had never said anything nasty to me, in fact his only fault seemed to be his taste in girlfriends. He'd had a few and they all seemed to be dumber than a dumb box of frogs.

I looked at my watch.

"Crap, come on, we only have five minutes until registration."

Jen and Annabel groaned and we hurried out of Starbucks, hot chocolates in our hands, and made our way to school.

Aberdeen is a mountain of grey granite buildings and the road our school was on featured some of the largest examples. The school itself was a huge mammoth building with beautiful carved windows. The front garden was immaculate with huge towering trees giving it the stature and appearance that a private school warrants. I always marvelled at its beauty even though I had attended the school for three years.

The building had been added to over the years, but the 'modern' extensions were all at the back so the face of the school remained old and historic.

As we entered I breathed in the familiar aroma of the buffed corridors before I started to tell them about a mammoth shopping trip I'd been on the week before with mum.

"So after I got my school stuff mum took me to the sale in New Look and holy pants, they had a whole rail of three pound stuff. I was in heaven. I got this really cute…"

My words were cut off as I walked into a wall.

I looked up to find the wall was actually Brandon grinning down at me, looking all lovely with his pale soft eyes. Mmmmmmmmmm.

"Sounds interesting," he laughed.

I took a step back and tried to stop blushing. His current girlfriend, a tall blonde waif called Britney of all things, snorted at me in a very unlady-like fashion and jangled her pink fluorescent bangles (I hoped they were confiscated). I gave her the evils in return.

"Erm, I'm sorry," I finally managed.

"No probs Rox see you in maths, we've got double period this afternoon."

He gave me a cheeky wink and started up the corridor. I stared after him and ignored the lingering glare from Britney. Once Brandon was out of sight Jennifer and Annabel burst into hysterics.

"He's as solid as a rock," I replied still a little dazed.

"I bet you did that on purpose," Annabel laughed.

"Ye cuz I want to make myself look like a total nerd in front of the school's hottest commodity."

Help my Granda is Haunting Me!

"Ooooooooooo," they both replied.

Chapter 2

Registration was a Brandon-free zone, as was English and geography, but maths wasn't. As I entered, arms linked with Jennifer, I saw him already sat in the row behind me, close enough to jab me with his pencil which he regularly did when he didn't know the answer to something. He gave me another cheeky grin and I tried not to look like a total geek.

Our teacher entered, a Mr Robinson who was from London. His accent made maths all the more enjoyable, he sounded like he should be selling stuff out of a suitcase down the market instead of teaching maths. We often tried to mimic it but it always sounded wrong - horribly wrong.

Today his accent was far from amusing because I'd hardly been in my seat thirty seconds when it said my name.

"Roxanne you're to report to the main office right away," his voice was deadly serious.

"Oh, is something wrong?"

The whole class was now looking and I shifted uncomfortably in my seat.

"Nothing you've done, just take your bag and report to reception."

Help my Granda is Haunting Me!

The receptionist was a young woman of stocky build, frizzy unruly red hair and a freckled complexion. She peered at me over the rim of her black framed glasses and seemed immediately inconvenienced by my presence.

"Er, Mr Robinson said I had to report here."

"Ah, Roxanne McDonald." Her posture instantly changed and her face softened into a look of sympathy.

"Mrs Abbott will be right out, just take a seat."

"Erm, OK."

Now I was really beginning to worry. I plonked myself down in a high-backed leather seat at the window. I'd either done something really wrong or something had gone wrong. A whole manner of stupid fictitious reasons came pouring into my head. Maybe I was being expelled or maybe...

"Come along Miss McDonald," my headmistress appeared and barked at me. I stood up quickly and followed closely behind.

Mrs Abbott was in her late fifties and had been teaching when being a teacher meant something more than someone who taught. In her day they had influence and respect, and she never tired of telling students this. She must have been pretty stunning when she was younger though, you could just tell. She always dressed impeccably, usually a tweed suit even in the height of summer, and she always wore pearls and a brooch. Today it was a small gold ladybird with red stones and her suit was a cream ensemble with a matching skirt that cut off below the knee. Her entire wardrobe looked like it had been bought from the Edinburgh

Woollen Mill (I don't shop there but my Nana loves it). I stared at the back of her impeccably styled hair as we made our way out of the school and into the car park. Mrs Abbott had a reserved parking space right outside the front door so we didn't have far to go.

"Miss?" I asked.

"Now your mother asked me to bring you directly home and I have been given instructions to do just that, nothing more."

"But do you know what's the matter? Is it bad?"

"Best you just see your mother dear."

Her face softened slightly and I got in the passenger seat, buckled my belt and stared at the car's dashboard clock to pass the time. Our flat was literally five minutes walk away from the school and it seemed pretty pointless being driven but I kept my mouth shut. My mum obviously wanted me home ASAP. In hardly any time at all we pulled up outside my apartment block, I released my seat belt and opened the car door.

"Thanks Mrs Abbott."

"No problem dear," she answered with a smile.

I didn't want to open the front door. I paused outside, gave Mrs Abbott a final farewell smile and pulled my key out of my blazer pocket; I then entered with a big sigh. Our flat was on the top floor and the climb seemed to take forever that day. I opened our front door and went straight into the living room to find mum sat on the sofa with her head in her hands crying.

"Mum, what's wrong?"

My mother looked up startled for a second like she'd forgotten where she was.

"Honey, you're home, oh it's terrible." She got up and hugged me fiercely.

"Mum please tell me what's going on?"

"It's your Granda honey, he died this morning."

"What?" I said in total disbelief. I actually thought at first I had heard wrong.

"He had a heart attack this morning and it was too much, he died in the ambulance on the way to the hospital."

My mum broke out into fresh sobs. I sank onto the edge of the sofa and frowned in disbelief. I had always been really close to my grandparents. Like me, my mum was an only child, so my grandparents had always been closely involved with our lives. I spent weekends out at their cottage in the country and when I was little they came to babysit if mum had planned a night out.

I tried to imagine a world without my Granda in it and I couldn't. He was there always with jokes, advice or criticism, usually criticism but it was always light-hearted and in jest. What was I going to do without him?

As an ex-navy officer who worked in the engine rooms, he had brash attitude and would yell obscenities at other drivers that got in his way. And although he loved young children, he hated teenagers - with the exception of me. He even looked like a proper Granda with a head of white wild hair and a big round belly that even at fifteen I loved to wrap my arms around. Not anymore. That was at an end. It was devastating news and yet I could not find it in me to shed a single tear. It did not make sense, it didn't seem real. Mum snuggled up next to me and we cuddled up together for a few minutes.

"Shall I make you a cup of tea mum?"

She nodded through her tears and I padded through to the kitchen. I added a teabag and an extra sugar to a mug while I waited for the kettle to finish taking its time and boil. I made it the way she liked it, strong with just a drop of milk. I took it back through to her and she placed it on the coffee table then just stared into space.

"Mum, you OK? Can I get you anything else?"

"No honey. I have to go and pick nana up from the hospital in a minute."

"I'll come with you."

"No Roxy, she's pretty inconsolable, I think I'll bring her back here."

"If you're sure. I'll just go to my room."

In a daze I went through to my bedroom and sat at the vanity table staring at my reflection in the mirror. I heard mum fish her keys out of the fruit bowl on the kitchen table before she walked along the hall and stopped at my door.

"I'll be back soon love, will you be OK?

I told her I'd be fine and listened as she left. I turned my attention back to my reflection. Why wasn't I crying? My Granda was dead, gone. I cried when I watched the *Lion King* and I was terrible with reunions on chat shows, but I couldn't shed a single tear for my beloved Granda who thought the world of me. It was an insult to his memory. I just had this horrible empty feeling inside, like I was void of emotions.

I didn't notice the swift passage of time but I heard my mum and nana open the front door and enter the flat. I turned and glanced at the clock on my bedside cabinet. A whole hour had passed and I'd just sat there staring at myself. A few seconds later my bedroom door opened and mum popped her head in.

"You OK Roxy love?"

"Aye mum."

"I'm just getting nana settled. She's going to sleep with me. Just shout if you need me OK."

Chapter 3

The following days were slow, mundane and trance-like. My mum and nana frequently hugged and cried. They constantly asked if I was OK and I always replied yes, but I wasn't. I was consumed with guilt. I tried and tried to summon the need to grieve and cry like everyone around me seemed to do. Once people found out Nana was staying with us they arrived in droves. I didn't know most of them so I stuck to my bedroom and kept my head down.

I found myself sat on the morning of Granda's funeral at my vanity table once more. I was wearing a new black dress and jacket, and everything was in place. Everything except the fact that it still didn't feel like he was dead, my head didn't believe it and my heart didn't believe it either.

I had to face facts; he was gone. My beloved Granda was dead and he was never coming back. I thought fondly of all the trips around Scotland we had taken when I was little. First in their caravan and then they'd upgraded to a motorhome. Wonderful times when I'd felt as though I was the centre of their world, and I had been. Granda had indulged my every whim to the point of spoiling me and it had driven mum crazy.

I felt my eyes welling up.

I thought of another time when we had gone to Landmark, an adventure park in the Highlands, and Granda, then in his sixties, had gone on a zip wire. I had laughed so hard it was actually sore. Afterwards nana cooked up a batch of bacon butties in the motorhome.

A small tear ran down my cheek.

I remembered offering to weed Granda's flower bed when I was about ten years old. I unknowingly dug up all his bulbs and even a few flowers too. Granda had simply laughed, he never really got mad at me.

Now my tears were unstoppable and they sploosh splooshed off the glass surface of the vanity table. How could I even begin to imagine a life without my Granda in it. I wanted so badly to hug him and tell him how much I loved him.

"Don't cry petal." The voice was soft like a whisper but unmistakably Granda's. My brow frowned at how real it had been. I reached down into my bottom drawer to get a tissue to dab my eyes.

"It'll be OK, don't worry." There it was again, only louder, closer.

I sat up straight and glanced into the mirror.

Stood there in the reflection was Granda, looking real and solid and definitely not deceased. I screamed and toppled backwards off my chair. I quickly got to my feet but he was gone. My heart was hammering in my chest and I tried to control my breathing. I put my hands out to steady myself because I felt quite faint.

My bedroom door burst open.

"Roxy!" mum shouted "What's the matter?"

"Erm, nothing. It was a spider."

"For the love of God, have I not got enough to worry about?"

"I'm sorry mum."

Her face softened a little.

"You want me to get it."

"Nah I got it."

"Well the car will be here in an hour."

"Yes mum."

The bedroom door was shut quietly leaving me stood shaking in the middle of my room wondering what to do next.

"Hello," I whispered loudly.

Nothing.

"Granda?"

Silence.

"Maybe I imag….."

"What?" The reply was muffled and came from inside my wardrobe.

"Is that you Granda?"

"Aye."

"Well come out, I can't talk to a wardrobe."

"No. I don't want to scare you."

"Gees Granda, of course I was gonna be scared. What reaction did you want?"

"I didn't think you'd see me. No one else can."

"No one?"

"No."

"Granda please come out."

I mentally prepared myself. A foot clad in a brown moccasin slipper appeared through the wardrobe door, followed by familiar grey sweatpants, yellow sleeveless shirt until finally there he stood. His grey hair was just as unruly. His arms were clad in old faded navy tattoos and he had a small tea stain down the front of his crisp shirt.

"Granda," I said full of love.

"Pet."

"You're a, a…ghost," the last word was a quiet whisper.

"Yes."

I felt that I should probably be a little more scared than I was but he didn't look like a ghost he just looked like my Granda; he just looked normal. He also looked as if he were waiting for me to freak out at any given moment.

"It's fine Granda. I'm fine. How long have you been…here?"

"I appeared in the ambulance on the way to the hospital."

"Oh Granda it must have been horrible."

We took a seat side by side on my bed. It sank slightly as I sat on it but nothing moved as Granda sat down, the covers remained puffed up. I put a hand out and gently reached out to touch his arm. My fingertips passed through, the air inside him felt cooler.

"What does it feel like, being dead?"

"Like I'm here, alive, except I can't touch anything."

"It sounds horrible."

"It was, well until now. It's better now you can see me."

"And I take it you stuck in them clothes?"

"Yes."

"Slippers and a tea stain for all time, eh, Granda?" I chuckled.

"Ya wee monkey!"

With the ice broken we chatted as if nothing had happened. All I could think was 'my Granda is here. I don't have to lose him and having him as a ghost is better than not having him at all'.

I tried to keep my voice down so that mum and Nana didn't think I'd gone insane and call Cornhill Mental Hospital. But sometimes it was hard to stifle the laughter, especially when Granda walked through the wall into next door's flat and came back even paler saying the woman was having a shower and he'd accidentally walked in on her. He asked how school was and I told him I hadn't even done a full day of the new school year.

"Sorry about that petal."

"Don't be sorry it's not like you could have helped it."

"I know but still, I'm here the now and I'm not going anywhere."

It was good to have him back

An hour later, Granda was sprawled on my bed and I was sat at my dressing table with my feet propped up on the bed. We were still chattering away like nothing had happened when mum knocked softly on my door. I grabbed my mobile as a cover story in case she'd heard me talking to Granda.

"The car is here sweetheart, it's time to go."

The funeral, how could I have forgotten about the bloomin' funeral?

"OK, mum I'll be right down."

Once the door was safely shut I turned back to Granda.

"I can't go to your funeral."

"Course you can. I'll come with you."

"You want to go to your own funeral? Isn't that…weird?"

"What, you mean weirder than me being here in the first place?"

"Fair enough."

The car that took us was lovely and posh. I sat in the back with mum and nana, while Granda took the front passenger seat by simply passing through the door. He even instinctively went for his seat belt then stopped when he realised his hand was passing through it. The mood in the back was suitably sombre and I decided my best option was to keep my head down, after all I was far from sombre, I was happy to have my Granda back. We drove out to the small funeral home and took our place behind the hearse. Then we made the slow but short journey to the church.

"Bonnie flowers," Granda said. "Lots of 'em too."

When I didn't respond Granda whipped round in his seat.

"I said bonnie flowers."

I looked at him desperately and motioned with eyes towards mum and nana.

"Oh sorry. I forgot."

He turned back round. A couple of school kids were playing by the side of the road.

"Have you no respect ya wee hooligans?" he shouted. "I remember a day where you stopped and bowed your head when a funeral car went by. Honestly." He shook his fist through the window and I bit my lip to stop from laughing.

We soon pulled up outside the quaint country church with its small cemetery and we followed the coffin inside and took our seats. There were a surprising amount of people inside and nearly all the seats were taken. Granda had been well liked and even though he and Nana had had a quiet retirement it was nice to know he was obviously well thought of. The coffin bearers brought the casket to the front of the church and then opened the top half. I hadn't realised it was to be an open casket. Thank God from where I was sat I couldn't see inside, I hadn't wanted to go and see him at the funeral home. This didn't seem to bother Granda though and he got up to have a nosey at what was going on inside. A crumbly old vicar appeared from the side and made his way to his little pew just to the side of the coffin.

"We are gathered here on this sombre…"

"I don't believe it!" Granda's voice boomed loudly over the vicars, echoing around the church unheard to everyone except me.

"They are burying me in me kilt."

"Finlay Crerar McDonald was a fine man."

"Not just any kilt…….my Pride of Scotland kilt!"

"A wise and patient man."

"It's only six months old. Really why don't you just take six hundred quid and shove it…"

I felt my face flame red as a string of obscenities straight from his days in the navy came flooding out of his mouth.

"He loved his family dearly."

"Here I am in my flaming slippers and tea-stained shirt and a perfectly good kilt is wasted."

"He would certainly be smiling now if he could see how many people came today….."

"My sporran! MY SILVER SPORRAN!"

"He is in the hands of God now and God will take care of him."

"No he bloody won't."

I raised my hands up to my mouth in shock and mum put a protective arm around me thinking I was upset. I concentrated hard and blocked everything out, both the monotonous tone of the vicar and the animated boom of Granda's voice which continued to sound out over the vicar throughout the whole service.

Luckily afterwards I was offered the choice of either going home or going to the wake. I chose home and was so relieved to be back in the confines of my familiar bedroom. Mum asked if I was going to be OK, then she left to keep Nana company.

I didn't have to wait long before Granda materialised through the door. At least we were alone in the flat and I didn't have to worry about whispering.

"Granda you have to be careful," I said seriously.

"What do you mean petal?"

"Well because I had to fight back the urge to talk to you, and was there any need for the obscenities in the church?"

"Maybe not."

"Nana put you in your kilt because she had fond memories of you in it and what was she going to do with it, eh?"

"You're right."

"From now on you have to be careful please, so I don't end up looking like a loon that talks to herself, OK?"

"OK, OK."

"Right, oh, and there's no way you are coming to school."

"But."

"No buts. School is a no-no."

"I'll be bored."

"Well go haunt someone, anyone, just not me. It's hard enough to fit in."

Chapter 4

The next day I decided to get my butt back to school. I awoke half an hour before my alarm was due to go off. I padded through to the bathroom and took a long hot shower which gave me time to think about the weirdness of the previous day. Once I was thoroughly washed and my hair was squeaky clean, I dried, dressed and did my hair. My hair is really, really thick and straight, and it seems to like holding onto moisture so it takes a good twenty minutes of blasting with a hairdryer to be bone dry. Then there's the fringe issue. My hair really doesn't like having a side parting one bit. Luckily even after all that, I had a good ten minutes to spare so I texted my two friends to let them know I was going back to school and then I decided I'd go and make my breakfast. I'd reached for the door handle when I heard Granda's voice from the other side.

"Roxanne is it safe to come in pet?"

An arm, clad in old navy tattoos suddenly appeared through my door, right in front of my face. I took a step back and watched it for a few seconds waving back and forth. What the bloomin' heck had happened in the last twenty-four hours that that didn't even phase me?

"It fine," I whispered and opened the door. "Morning Granda, I need to get breakfast. Annabel and Jennifer will be here soon."

"OK," he whispered back. "You sure I can't come with you, I promise I'll be..."

"No!" I interrupted "...and why are you whispering?"

"I don't know," he said in his normal tone.

I shook my head, smiled at him and went through to the kitchen.

"Morning honey," mum greeted. "Roxy you don't have to go back to school yet honey. Take a few more days off if you like."

"No mum, it's fine. I don't want to fall behind and besides there's big exams this year."

"OK honey. You want me to do you some toast?"

"Yes please."

I ate my toast and waited downstairs for Annabel and Jennifer. They appeared at the bottom of the road and sped up slightly when they saw I was waiting.

"I'm sorry about your grandpa Rox," Annabel said when they reached me. They both gave me hugs.

"Thanks."

"You OK?" Jennifer added.

"I'm fine guys, OK. Don't worry," I smiled to reassure them. "So what's happened while I've been away?"

"We have a new maths teacher," Jennifer said blushing slightly.

"Oh what's he like?"

"Well he's kinda…"

"Jennifer has it bad," Annabel laughed, interrupting. "I even wish I had advanced maths so I could get a look in."

"You hate maths," Jennifer exclaimed.

"Yes but if I'd known the teacher was that hot I'd have studied harder."

"He's that nice, huh? I came back just in time me."

We grabbed our usual hot chocolate and made our way to school. I felt a little bad at banning Granda from accompanying me to school but he wasn't the sort of person to sit in a corner and not be heard. I just hoped he wouldn't be too bored.

As we entered the car park Brandon was just getting out of the passenger seat of a huge four-by-four. He slammed the door, waved when he saw us, then bounded over. Holy cow, he looked like an advert for a shampoo brand. His hair bounced majestically and he looked soooooo good. I stopped drooling (not literally) and smiled as he reached us.

"Hi Roxanne," he said.

"Erm, hi Brandon."

"I just wanted to say, Jennifer told me about your grandad and I'm real sorry."

I was a little stunned. He was the nicest looking, most popular boy at school and he'd gone out of his way to console me. He looked totally genuine too. Brandon reached out and patted the side of my arm.

"Thanks," I replied.

"No probs, I'll see you in maths. The new guy is really cool."

I sighed as I watched him walk away and ran my hand over my arm where he had patted me. As he walked he casually ran his fingers through his hair. A girl, a different one from the last time I saw him, caught up with him and linked arms. It was so unfair.

"I'm not the one who's got it bad," Jennifer laughed.

"Shut up guys," I slapped Jen playfully on the shoulder. "He is lovely though."

"Wait till you meet Mr Winters."

We had maths straight after dinnertime registration and by then I had been well filled in on Mr Winters. I knew he had long thick hair tied back and he always wore a tailored suit. His eyes were the colour of the sea, he liked beef sandwiches and his lips were like two soft fluffy pillows, apparently. In fact the only thing I didn't know was his shoe size although Jennifer told me his feet were huge. Annabel was right, Jennifer had it bad. I figured it would definitely be a good thing for me to have a distraction from thinking about Brandon.

We sat in maths and I was practically on the edge of my seat waiting for this Adonis to arrive but when he entered I was hugely disappointed. He was a good-looking man but I didn't fancy him. When I turned to Jennifer, who was starry starry-eyed and told her, she scoffed noisily at me.

"You have no taste woman."

The noise level briefly picked up amongst the female students in the room until Mr Winters shushed everyone.

"Ah, you must be Miss McDonald," he said once everyone had settled down.

"Yes sir."

"Well Miss McDonald we started brushing up on our algebra. Page forty-two of the text book if you please. There was supposed to be a mock test today. Do you want to attempt it?"

"Yes sir. That should be fine." His voice had a very fatherly, soothing tone and I found myself warming to his teaching methods immediately.

It was lucky that maths was my favourite subject. It's what made me a geek and the butt of the occasional joke. I heard a snigger from the back of the class and a loud cough muffling the word, swot. I then heard Brandon telling his new, lesser half to quit it. I smiled at his gesture.

Maths was actually a lot more enjoyable with Mr Winters teaching. He talked to us students as if he were talking to other adults instead of a bunch of fifteen year olds. He had a way of describing things which made then so easy to understand. Jennifer stared at him in absolute awe for the whole lesson and I couldn't help but snicker now and again. The test was a breeze. Maths made sense to me and it always had. Some people are gifted with art and music, I was gifted with numbers. I was destined from an early age to be geekalious. Mr Winters marked them while we did some further exercises then he handed them back to us.

"Jennifer, not bad twenty-five out of thirty." She might have well have grasped the paper to her chest she looked so happy with his compliment.

He continued handing out the papers giving little comments and criticism where due.

"Brandon Heathly, ten out of thirty. Did you study the extra work I gave you?"

"Yes sir, I just find it difficult."

"No matter, we'll persevere, OK?"

"Thanks sir."

"Roxanne, well done twenty-nine out of thirty and with no prior revision too."

Again came snorting noises from the back.

"For God's sake Tiff," I heard Brandon hiss.

"Now Wednesday is double maths and we'll be studying Pythagoras. Read up people."

The bell went and everyone packed their bags. I noticed Jennifer took her time making sure everything was packed neatly away in her bag. I rolled my eyes at her and she hurried up so we could get to our next class.

"Brandon, Roxanne, stay behind a moment please."

Puzzled I looked at Brandon. He looked equally as baffled as I.

"Come here please."

We both approached his desk.

"Now, Brandon I didn't want to say in front of all the class but you really need extra help on your maths my boy or we may have to think about dropping you out of advanced."

"I know sir," he agreed, wincing slightly.

"Now Roxanne is a straight 'A' maths student and if she's willing, and has the time, it might be an idea for her to coach you."

"Me!" I gasped.

"Yes you. Now I know you have a lot with playing rugby Brandon, so let's have a look at your timetables and see if we can work out a couple of hours a week for extra study. What do you both think?"

There was silence, an awkward one, and I was sure it was because it was probably the last thing Brandon wanted to do.

"Well," Brandon finally said. "I mean if you don't mind Rox, I'd really appreciate it."

I smiled. I tried not to smile too wide. Be cool, I told myself.

"Sure." I reached into my bag and dug out my timetable. My hand was shaking slightly as I handed it over. Mr Winters looked over them.

"OK, well it looks like you both have a study period on a Friday afternoon, so as long as you are both up to date with everything else you could use that. Now Brandon, you don't have anything on a Tuesday after school, so if Roxy doesn't mind spending some time in the library that would be great. If you did an hour both days, till Brandon has caught up, that would be super. How does that sound?"

We both nodded.

"It would be a shame to move you out of the advanced Brandon. You were top of the class last year. You'd best go to your next classes guys. Thanks Roxy."

"Erm, no problem," I replied in a total daze.

He gave me a grateful smile and we walked out of class together. Brandon's girlfriend, Tiffany was waiting for him outside the class.

"What's up baby?" she said in an annoying high-pitched voice - eurgh! Her hair was tied up with a backcombed quiff at the front.

"I'll tell you later, I've got to get to gym class," Brandon replied.

I didn't need to listen to the two of them bantering on so I decided to get to my next class.

"I'll walk you babes OK?" she squeaked.

"Sure, catch you later Rox," he called out.

I turned, raised my hand and gave him a nod and he smiled back

"And thanks, you're a life-saver."

When I was round the corner out of their sights I let a big stupid grin spread across my face. Two whole hours a week with Brandon all to myself coaching him on my favourite subject. Oh my God, oh my God. He had seemed genuinely pleased I was helping him out too. Perhaps there was hope for all us geeks out there.

Chapter 5

I made a detour to the toilets and looked in the mirror. I tilted my head from side to side to see if there was anything different about me that day. Maybe this was my lucky year. In my wildest of wild dreams I always imagined Brandon and I as an item. Was this a small glimmer of hope? He was so nice to me usually it was really hard to tell if he was flirty nice or friendly nice.

"Ring a ring o'roses, a pocketful of posies, atishoo, atishoo, we all fall down."

The voice was coming from the other end of the toilets.

"Hello?" I called out.

"Ally, bally, ally bally bee, sittin' on yer mammy's knee, greetin' for anether bawbee, tae buy mair Coulter's candy."

As the voice sang I traced its source to the end cubicle. It was a really sad young child's voice.

"Anyone there?" I knocked lightly on the door.

Nothing.

The cubicle door was slightly ajar so I inched it open. It was empty.

I turned, feeling puzzled and came face to face with a blonde girl who looked about three or four years younger than me. She stood looking at me as if I was a two-headed green monster.

Something still wasn't right. The girl looked OK; she was a thin, pretty thing, but she wasn't wearing her school uniform.

"You scared the b-jesus out of me!" I told her.

"You can see me?"

Then it clicked. I looked again at her clothes. She was wearing a pinafore, a blue and white chequered thing, heavy black shoes and frilled ankle socks, something a schoolgirl would have worn many, many years ago.

"You have got to be kidding me," I said in disbelief. The girl was suddenly animated.

"You can see me, you can hear me!"

"Yes I can see you."

"You have to help me."

"What do you mean I have to help you?"

"So I can leave this place. Please help me."

"This place, you mean you're stuck here at school."

"No here on earth."

"I don't know if I can," I replied honestly.

"But I'm the last one. Everyone else has gone."

"What do you mean?"

The girl lowered her voice to a whisper.

"He murdered us, the headmaster, Mr Ratchet."

"Mr Ratchet? I've never heard of…"

"He's coming, I have to go…"

"What do you mean he's coming?"

The girl disappeared with a pop and in the next instant a wind picked up in the toilets. My hair was blown wildly in all directions and bits of square loo paper blew like a white hurricane around me. I couldn't see but I knew the general direction of the door so I ran towards it. I wrenched it open when I found the handle and fell out into the corridor.

Silence. I smoothed down my hair and skirt, and picked a couple of stray pieces of toilet paper from my uniform.

"Great," I muttered. "I've turned into a medium."

I glanced around the empty corridor nervously. When my heart had stopped pounding inside my chest and my hands had stopped shaking, I made my way to my next and last class of the day, English.

I explained to my teacher, Miss Stuart about being kept behind in maths, then took my seat next to Annabel and filled her quietly in about tutoring Brandon. I missed out the toilet incident.

"That is soooooo cool," she whispered excitedly.

"Quiet there, come on girls. Read pages fifteen through to thirty, in silence."

Miss Stuart, looked like she was at least seventy. She had retired once but due to a lack of teachers she had come back on a temporary basis. Her hair was always neatly tied in a steel white bun and she always wore long flowery skirts with a white or cream silk blouse.

She knew everything there was to know about Aberdeen. She had never set a foot outside it and was proud of telling everyone so. If someone got burgled, she knew their neighbour. If someone was murdered she'd heard all the details before the press got them.

'Wait a minute,' I thought. Old nosy Miss Stuart, never set foot outside Aberdeen and knew everything. I had a plan. I waited until the end of class and promised to catch up to Annabel in the canteen.

"Erm, Miss Stuart, I was wondering if I could ask you something?"

"Of course dear was it about *Of Mice and Men*?"

"No, I was just wondering if you knew of a headmaster at this school. A Mr Ratchet?"

The colour drained from her face and she took a seat.

"Miss Stuart, are you OK?"

"Why do you ask Roxanne?"

"It was just something my nana mentioned and I thought, seeing as you're so knowledgeable about Aberdeen history, I thought you might have heard about him."

"I was a pupil here when he was headmaster."

"So he was real?" I was shocked.

"Yes and he still haunts my dreams to this day."

"So it's true, he murdered some children."

"He murdered five little girls in the forties and then when the police cottoned on to him he took his own life in the very basement of this school."

"How horrible."

"They found the bodies of five of the girls; one is still missing to this day."

I was totally gobsmacked.

"Carrie Anne Mackie was her name. We were good friends too."

"I'm sorry Miss."

Miss Stuart had drifted off into a daydream.

"Sometimes I swear I hear the click-click of his heals in the corridor."

I backed away to the doorway, fumbled for the handle and left feeling slightly guilty. I stepped back into the corridor pulled my bag onto my shoulder and headed off to meet Annabel as I had promised. It was the longest walk of my life even though it was only three corridors away. I kept expecting Carrie Ann to appear or Mr Ratchet to whip more toilet roll at me.

Jennifer was with Annabel and they were obviously chatting about Brandon. I knew because they both stood with stupid grins on their faces.

"You guys," I said. "They are gonna lock you up if you don't pull your faces straight. You look like a pair of goons."

"He likes you," Jennifer said.

"Honestly, I'm just giving him extra tuition. He's seeing that waif Tiffany."

Annabel rightly snorted and we made our way out of the school and set off for home.

The house was empty when I arrived back home. I knew mum had booked an extra week off work so I figured she was probably out at nana's. I grabbed my *Heat magazine* from my dressing table and went to the bathroom. I realised I was probably never going to have the courage to use the school toilet again. I sat down and leafed through the fashion pages while I did my business.

"He's always there you know."

"Ahhhhhhhhhhhhhhhhhhhhhhhh," I let out a high pitched scream as the ghost Carrie Anne popped in front of me.

"Oh sorry. I didn't mean to scare you," she said timidly.

"Gees, I'm on the toilet."

"Oh."

"Can you at least go wait in my bedroom?"

"Ok, where is it?"

"It's right next door, here," I tapped on the wall to my left and she walked through it. I decided before I dealt with the ghost I needed chocolate, big time. There was a note on the fridge from mum, she was spending time at nana's and she would be home later. There were ready meals in the fridge and I wasn't to go out anywhere without ringing first. I wondered idly if Granda had gone with them. I grabbed a Mars Bar and a can of diet Irn Bru and padded through to my bedroom where Carrie Anne was sitting on my bed staring at the posters on my wall.

"This is a nice room," she said to me innocently.

"Can the other ghost follow you here?"

"What other ghost?"

"Mr Ratchet, who else?"

I took a seat at my vanity table and devoured my Mars Bar.

"He isn't a ghost. He is an essence."

"A what?" I talked with my mouth open. I'd gone beyond manners.

"It's a little bit of evil left over from the bad things he did."

"So can it come here?"

"No it's tied to the building where he died."

"But you aren't."

"No, but I have to go back there. I can't stay away for too long, ever."

"Oh."

I looked at the poor little girl. "I'm sorry you died Carrie."

"How do you know my name?"

"I spoke to Miss Stuart, she was your friend I believe."

Carrie's eyes started to water.

"She was a good friend; we used to walk to school together every day. The day I died she was ill at home with the chicken pox. She blamed herself. She goes to the cemetery where they put up a stone for me and she speaks to me. She says she's sorry. She thinks if she'd been at school that day then Mr Ratchet wouldn't have seen me leaving alone and well…"

"I wondered why she went funny when I asked her, how sad. Well I can try to help you, but I'm kind of new to this. I've only been seeing ghosts since yesterday. My Granda died last week and I saw him for the first time yesterday."

"I did wonder why you hadn't seen me before. I've seen you."

"OK, that's creepy."

"You like that boy don't you; the one with the brown hair and the pretty eyes?"

"OK, quiet you."

"I think he likes you too."

"Now you're just talking crazy. Have you seen him? Have you seen me?"

"You're really pretty."

"Look we're going way off topic here. Tell me how can I help you?"

"It's simple, they need to find me."

"They need to…what? You want me to help find a dead body."

"It's the only way for me to find peace; it's what I want most."

"Do you know where it is?"

"No. I just know it's somewhere in the school."

"Great. Fabulous."

I got up and paced the floor a little.

"So I have to find the body of a dead girl, murdered, what fifty years ago?"

"Sixty-one years ago."

"You don't know where you were buried and the only person who does know is an essence floating around a school toilet."

"That's pretty much it."

"Peachy. Maybe my Granda can help. I dunno where he is though. He might have gone with my mum back to nanas."

"I'm in the wardrobe," came a muffled voice.

"Granda what are you doing in there?"

He stepped out and stood in the middle of the room.

"Well this keeps getting weirder by the minute," I said.

"I heard you come in then tell someone to go wait in your room. I thought it was one of your friends so I hid."

"Granda this is Carrie, Carrie this is my Granda. I'm assuming you can see each other yes?"

They both nodded.

"Great. Wait this is great. You two can keep each other company. Carrie you can stay here OK."

"I can't stay away too long. The essence gets restless."
"And?"

"He will cause ill feeling"

"Oh, but that doesn't sound too bad."

"It has the power to transmit negative emotions but if I am there, close by, he is relatively calm."

"How bad can it be?"

"If I'm gone for longer than a few hours people can start to get aggressive towards each other."

"Ah that explains why Tiffany Matthews was such a cow to me last year."

"Matthews," Carrie said thinking "Is that the thin girl with the strange hair? All puffed up at the front."

I laughed.

"Yes that's her."

"Nope, she's just a cow," she smiled cheekily.

"Oh, well I did have my suspicions."

"You didn't tell me someone was mean to you," Granda said, sounding slightly hurt.

"She's mean to everyone Granda."

"She is now hanging around with that boy you like," Carrie said.

"Roxy, what boy is this?"

"No one. Quiet you," I pointed at Carrie then quickly got back on topic.

"Right OK, how about this? Granda can you keep Carrie company? You'll have to go and hang around school with her and I'll try to figure out where I even begin to start with this whole mess."

"I remember when those murders happened," Granda said.

"You do!" Me and Carrie said at the same time.

"Yes, well I was only ten. But you don't forget things like that in a hurry."

"Spill it," I said. "Tell us what you know."

"Well Mr Ratchet had been headmaster for a number of years. The school was an all-girl's school at the time. They all said he was too strict with girls there and some parents pulled their children out. Then over a period of about seven months, five girls went missing. Then a sixth girl went missing and they found her at Mr Ratchet's mansion on Millionaire's Row. She barely survived. He'd arrived home and seen all the police and legged it. Knowing his number was up he returned to the school, went to the basement and…well he hanged himself."

"So he didn't murder the girls at school?" Roxy asked.

"No, all the girls were murdered at his mansion and buried in the garden."

"Well maybe you're there too Carrie?"

"No, I died at school."

"Are you sure?"

"Yes, in his office."

"In his…crap. Did he hurt you?" I was almost afraid to ask.

"No, he didn't mean to kill me, not so quick. He asked me if I'd like a lift home and I'd accepted. Only I got scared and said I was going to walk. He tried insisting, then he got angry with me. I tried to run and he grabbed me. He put his hand over my mouth to stop me screaming and that's all I remember."

"My God," my Granda said softly.

"I guess I'm lucky. If he'd got me back to his mansion it would have been a lot worse for me. He hurt the girls pretty bad."

"What a monster," I said. "Well I'll need to see if I can find the exact date you went missing. Then I'll have to find plans and see what else I can dig up. But we'll help you."

"Thank you so much. The other girls were there for a few days. They were tied to his essence you see but as they found their bodies the girls passed over until only I was left."

"And you've been on your own all this time?"

"Yes," Carrie suddenly looked faint. "I have to go back now."

"Granda, can you go with her? I don't like the thought of her being alone."

"Of course petal."

He reached out and offered Carrie his withered hand and to my surprise she was able to take it.

"I'll look after you. What a time you've had you poor bairn."

They walked hand in hand, disappeared through the bedroom door and I was left alone.

I made myself a hot chocolate and bunged a shepherd's pie in the microwave. While I waited for it to heat up I switched on the computer in the living room and Googled Mr Ratchet. I grabbed my steaming hot nutrious ready meal and then sat for the next hour making notes about him.

He was a vile and horrible man, a man who had enjoyed torturing little girls and had never been punished. Worse, he was still doing it. He was holding Carrie Anne, tying her to him even in death. I came across an old photo of his house and wondered if it was still standing and who lived in it now. When I found an actual photo of him I was shocked. He was a stocky man in his early forties with a heavy moustache, big sideburns and too close together eyes; his image made me shudder with fear to my very core. He looked evil, pure evil.

I did not sleep well that night, my dreams were haunted by Mr Ratchet and his beady eyes. I wish I hadn't read about the things he had been capable of. I wished Granda had stayed to watch over me but I was happy that he was with Carrie, the little girl needed him more. Finally in the early hours of the morning I fell asleep again, this one was blissfully dream free.

Chapter 6

My alarm buzzed me awake the next morning, I groaned and hit the snooze button. Three snoozes later I pulled myself out of bed and groaned a bit more. A glance in the mirror told me I could carry shopping in the bags under my eyes and my hair was a lost cause. No one ever looked at me anyway so who would care?

"Oh no!" I cried out loud suddenly remembering I was tutoring Brandon that day.

"Mum," I bellowed out of my bedroom door. "Can you plait my hair please?"

Mum popped her head out of the kitchen door.

"Sure honey, but I thought it was straight, straight straight!" She motioned with her hands to prove her point.

"No time."

"Well hurry, get dressed, brush your teeth. Your toast is on the table and I'll plait it while you eat, OK?"

"Thanks mum."

I yanked my uniform on and applied some lip gloss.

"Morning petal," said Granda materialising in the room.

"Morning Granda, I'm running really late. How was it last night?"

"Ghastly place to be at night, the poor girl. I've said I'll stay with her till we can free her though."

"That's nice Granda, but what if I can't."

"You will sweetheart I know you will."

I was pleased he had such confidence in me but I wasn't so sure.

"I'm gonna have to dash, I've got a fifteen minute break in between science and geography. So tell Carrie to meet me at the back of the library in the reference section."

"OK honey."

I gave him an air kiss and hurried to get breakfast and have my hair plaited.

My morning classes seemed to drag on and on, and I was ill at ease all the time. Buried, somewhere within the walls of my school was a little girl's body and it was up to me to help find it. I'd never seen a dead body before. The only person close to me to have died was Granda and I hadn't wanted to go and see him at the chapel of rest, I'd been too scared. I didn't suppose there would be much left of Carrie Anne to find but I still shuddered to think. I was wandering from class to class pondering my hopeless situation when I ran into Brandon.

"Hey Rox," he said "We still on for today?"

"Yes sure."

"Where do you want to do it?" he said cheekily and raised his eyebrows.

"Beg your pardon," I said still tired and distracted.

"Studying," he laughed.

I smiled back.

"How about the library, it stays open till five and I have some research I can be doing too."

"Cool, I can't thank you enough for helping me, I totally suck at maths."

"It's fine. Where's Tiffany?"

"Home ec."

An image came into my mind of Tiffany with her perfect nails and two hundred pound designer shoes cooking and I couldn't help but chuckle.

"She any good?" I asked.

"She burnt a boiled egg the other day."

I huge belly laugh escaped my lips.

"I'm not even joking," he joined in.

"I've got to dash," I said when I calmed down. I had never wanted to stay somewhere so much.

"Sure I have English. I'll see you at three thirty Rox."

He walked away, giving me a casual wave without looking back. I took a personal moment and tried to get a hold of myself. Once calm I made my way to the library to meet Granda and Carrie. Our school boasted one of the biggest and most well-stocked libraries of all the schools in Aberdeen, and the reference section was right at the back with a few comfy chairs. Very few students needed books from there so I'd suggested it knowing we weren't likely to get disturbed. Granda and Carrie were waiting for me sat in a couple of leather chairs, chatting away like they'd known each other forever. My Granda was like that. Everyone who knew him, loved him.

"Hi," I said smiling at the unlikely pair.

"Hi Roxy," Carrie replied.

"Hello there petal," Granda added.

I told them everything I had discovered the previous night on the internet.

"I'm just thinking that perhaps he wouldn't have taken you very far because there would have been a lot of people around, staff. The only problem is we don't know how much has changed since he was here. The layout of the school has probably been altered and added onto. I need to find as much information as I can about the school and the murder case."

"Well why don't you ask the librarian? There might be something in here to help you," Granda suggested.

"Good idea," I agreed. "I'm gonna have to get to my next class. I'm in the library after school because I'm tutoring Brandon."

Carrie grinned widely.

"As a favour to Mr Winters," I protested. She grinned even wider.

"Quiet you!"

When lunchtime came Annabel and Jennifer were glued to my side like barnacles. They were far too excited about my extra-curricular tutoring. OK, OK, I was excited too but I didn't want to show it. They spent the whole lunch hour coming up with elaborate stories about how Brandon was going to fall helplessly in love with me. Each story was more far-fetched than the last but at least my mind was occupied. Granda and Carrie stayed hidden, God knows what they were getting up to, so that meant my afternoon was ghost-free.

Art was the last lesson, another of my favourites. Annabel was in it with me, Jennifer wasn't because she had music but Brandon was, and unfortunately for me, his bit of fluff Tiffany. That day we were drawing a bowl of fruit. The fruit was placed in the centre of the room and we all sat around it. Annabel was next to me, Brandon and Tiffany directly opposite. Brandon gave me a little mini wave and a smile that did funny things to my knees and then he received a hard shove in the ribs from Tiffany.

"Ow, that hurt."

"You're supposed to be drawing."

"Like you you mean," he laughed warmly. "And what's that?" He pointed to Tiffany's page.

"My banana."

"It's oblong." He grinned cheekily at her.

"It's only a rough sketch at the minute." She jabbed him with the end of her pencil.

"Isn't she lucky," Annabel sighed.

"Yup." I agreed. "I have no idea what he sees in her or any of the others."

"It's arm candy. You have your stupid expensive designer school bag that you can't fit anything into, and he has Tiffany who can't fit anything into her head except simple simple thoughts."

"Annabel," I sniggered under my breath "That's so mean."

"So you disagree."

"Absolutely, my designer bag is totally fabulous it shouldn't be compared to her."

By the time the bell rang I was a total bag of nerves.

"I'll walk you to the library," Annabel said.

"OK."

Brandon gave me another wave as he gracefully packed away his belongings.

"I've just got to pick up my gym kit from my locker and I'll meet you there," he called over. "Sure," I replied. I then linked arms with Annabel in a cool fashion and made my way downstairs to the library.

"You have to call me tonight and tell me everything."

"I thought you'd studied pi?"

"Roxanne you know exactly what I mean. I want gossip, solid juicy gossip! Right, I'm gonna go and meet Jennifer. Skype me tonight if you can and tell us both everything."

"Fine, now go."

I shook my head at her and pushed open the door to the library.

"Hey you wait," I looked up to see Tiffany tottering down the stairs in heels I'm pretty sure she wasn't allowed to wear to school. I rolled my eyes and waited.

Tiffany took a long moment to catch her breath.

"I know what you're trying to do," she heaved.

"You know Tiffany, you should really stop smoking."
"Shut up you stupid little cow. I know you want him.
Every girl wants him. He's with me OK. He. Is. Mine.
Have you got it?"

"What. Ever. You. Say," I replied.

Tiffany's face flamed bright red and feeling slightly
awkward I took a step into the library to get away. She
grabbed my arm and stopped me.

"I don't know why I'm even worried, like he'd even want
you anyway. He laughs at you, you know. He's nice to
your face but laughs behind your back."

"Tiffany, if that were true, which I doubt, why are you
warning me to stay away and why the overdramatic
jealously display, huh?"

"Whatever frizzball, but you've been warned. You try
anything and you'll be sorry."

"Right well, thanks ever so much. Now take you hand
off me." I looked her square in the face.

I've never been the sort of girl to ever pick a fight and I
avoid confrontation wherever I can but I wasn't going to be
bullied or pushed around by anyone, especially Tiffany
flaming Matthews. With a humph she released her grip and
sauntered off with such a swagger that her bouffant bounced
up and down.

I headed over to the library reception and waited
patiently for someone to emerge from the back.

"Hi," the librarian said when she finally came through. "Can I help you?

She was young and pretty cool for a librarian which was fab because it meant that she tried to order all the latest books. She was really helpful and easy to talk to as well.

"Yes I'm doing an essay on local history and I want to centre it on the history of the school. Are there any books dating back say seventy or so years ago?"

"Hmm I think we do have quite a few local history books. I'll write down the aisle number and you'll have to browse through OK?"

"Sure."

"You'll probably get more from the microfilm."

"Microfilm?"

"It's a special machine that reads rolls of film with information on them, usually newspapers. We have a catalogue of all the Evening Express articles since it began in 1879."

"Really?"

"Yes, really. Although it's a lot to get through."

"I've never seen this microfilm thingy."

"They aren't as popular since the internet came about. It's stored through the back."

"Can you bring it out here?"

"It's too big but I can allow you some time through the back if you book well in advance and if you let me know some exact dates I'll look them out for you."

"Wow thanks that's really helpful."

"That's what I'm here for. If you can't find anything of use on that shelf then come back and see if I can spare you some time to help look."

"Thanks. Can I look at the microfilm on, say Thursday?"

"That sounds fine." She took a little square of yellow paper from under the counter and scribbled down a number "Here's the shelf with all the local history books on. See how you get on and come back. See me if you need anything else."

"Thank you."

I headed straight for the shelf number on my little piece of paper and began to browse. I heard a faint pop and Granda appeared quickly followed by Carrie.

"I can't speak for long. Brandon is coming in a minute," I whispered.

I told them about the microfilm. Carrie had no idea what it was but Granda was well up to speed. I betted that he knew more about the microfilm thingy than the brand new PC he bought from John Lewis three months ago that he had no idea how to work. He adored gadgets but didn't always know what to do with them once he bought them.

"We might find something in here to help us." I began browsing through the books to see if there was anything of interest.

"OK I think there's stuff here I can use. *Aberdeen - A History from 1800-2000*, that'll do, oooooo here's one, *Aberdeen Remembered*. Cool here's a good one, *Blood and*

Granite." I took the three books from the shelf and went to check them out.

"It's the first sign of madness you know." I bumped into Brandon at the end of the aisle.

I blushed the colour of a tomato and heard Granda and Carrie pop, pop away.

"What?" I stammered.

"Talking to yourself, it's the first sign of madness."

I laughed nervously.

"I was thinking aloud sorry."

"Don't be, I'm only kidding around with you."

"Just let me check these out and I'll be right with you. Why don't you get out your maths stuff?"

"Yes Miss." He grinned, gave me a salute and made his way over to the study area where he dumped his bag and began rummaging inside. I checked out my books and put them away. I gave the librarian the year I thought Mr Ratchet became headmaster, 1943 and I asked for the microfilm through to 1948.

Brandon had set out his maths book, pad, pen, ruler and triangles. I took a really deep breath and looked at him for a moment. He was so lovely it made my heart ache. What the heck was wrong with me? He had taken off his blazer and hooked it on the back of his chair.

'Get a hold of yourself Rox' I thought. I needed to be cool and level-headed because: A - he had a girlfriend; B - he was so far out of my league it was criminal; and C - I wouldn't have a clue what to do with him IF I got him. He seemed to sense me watching him, looked up and smiled.

"Where do you want to start?" I said slipping into the seat next to him.

"Hmmm, why don't we do half an hour of algebra and then do some Pythagoras."

"OK. Well why don't we go over yesterday's test, see where you went wrong. Then you can try some similar questions."

"Sounds good." He got his test out and I looked over it to see where he had gone wrong.

"I think you're just trying too hard at this. Strip it back to basics. Just because we are in advanced maths doesn't mean it's always going to be a complicated solution."

We went through the questions he had got wrong one by one, each time I explained how and why he slipped up. Then I tried to tell him how to rectify it.

"I actually think I'm getting this. Right test me oh mighty teacher of algebra!"

I laughed as I jotted some down, really pleased that he didn't seem at all bored. If fact he was really enthusiastic. I loved the drawl of his voice and the time flew by quickly and comfortably.

"I really think you've got the hang of it," I told him, "But we've only got twenty minutes until the library shuts so we'll have to do just a little on Pi today."

"But Mr Winters said for us to read up on it and I'm struggling with it."

"Well I mean, we could do some more if you haven't got anywhere to go, but we'll have to find somewhere else to study."

"How about Starbucks at the top of Union Street, my treat?"

"Sure, I live near there anyway."

"I'll just call Eric and tell him to pick me up a bit later."

We packed up our things and headed out into the school car park.

"Who's Eric?"

"My minder."

"Where are you parents?"

"They don't live here, they stay, abroad."

"Wow and they let you stay here, alone?"

"Yes, great isn't it?"

I gave mum a call on her mobile to let her know who I was with and why. Mum has always been really laid back with me but I don't give her any grief so she rarely has to raise her voice to me and trusted me totally.

"Will you be OK honey?"

"Yes, me and Brandon are heading for Starbucks for some extra study time but I'll be home well before six."

"You just be careful."

"Yes mum."

Brandon had called his minder by the time I'd hung up.

"Eric's a really cool guy, a friend of my dad's," he said holding the door to Starbucks open so I could enter.

"You fancy a piece of cake Rox? Look they have chocolate, wow four layers."

My stomach growled my answer.

"I think that's a yes," I said chuckling.

"You want hot chocolate too?"

"Chocolate overload."

"I have a real sweet tooth."

He ordered us both a slice of chocolate cake. The cake was covered in fudge icing sugar an inch thick to boot. He also ordered two full fat hot chocolates with all the trimmings. We found a table near the back that had a sofa instead of chairs and got out all our maths stuff again.

"I'm glad they turned this into a Starbucks," I said.

"Yes I hate McDonalds."

"Hey!"

"Ah, whoops, present company excepted."

"That's OK then."

We attacked Pythagoras with gusto and I tried not to look like I was having too good a time (maths wasn't meant to be fun was it?) but being with Brandon was too easy, if that made sense. It was like we met up everyday for hot chocolate and ridiculously tall cake. Brandon was a fast learner and he seemed really keen to absorb everything I was telling him. I looked at my watch and was shocked at how fast the evening had sped along, it was already six. We decided to call it a day.

"I'll walk you home."

"That's OK, it's only like, two streets away," I said.

"I insist. I've kept you later than we planned."

"If you're sure?"

"You still alright for Friday?"

"Of course. Let's see how you do tomorrow though you might not even need me."

The walk home only took five minutes and we chatted as we went along.

"I heard a rugby scout came to one of your matches last month," I said.

"He did indeed, how did you hear that?"

"I overheard someone talking about it in science the other week."

"He was impressed by my performance so it might open a few doors for me. My parents would prefer me to concentrate on more academic subjects though."

"But if you're good at something then you should take it as far as you can."

"My mom doesn't get sports."

"What does she do?"

"Not a lot," he laughed nervously.

"Sorry."

"Hey, don't you be sorry Rox."

"I'm prying."

"You're not prying anywhere I don't want you go." He smiled as if to reassure me.

Much to my disappointment we had reached my flat.

"Well this is me," I said pulling my keys out of my bag.

"Cool, well I'll see you tomorrow and thanks Roxy, I really appreciate it."

"No problem, anytime."

Chapter 7

I was totally on a high as I entered the main door. I flew up the four flights of stairs quickly, opened the front door and ran through to living room. I hurried over to the window to catch a little glimpse of him walking up the street but he had gone already. He was fast. I pouted a little to myself.

I headed for the kitchen, poured myself a nice cold glass of orange juice and made my way to my bedroom where, without so much as a rest from all the algebra, I got out the three history books and began leafing through trying to find relevant pieces about Mr Ratchet. I came across some old pictures of the school at around the time of the murders. The most helpful was *Blood and Granite*. There was a whole piece on Charles Emerson Ratchet. He had taught at the school since the mid thirties and took up the post as headmaster in summer 1943. The little girls started going missing in January 1948. Carrie Anne went missing on April 19, she was the fourth girl. The sixth girl, thirteen-year-old Valerie Drummer was discovered alive on August 12. There were several other pictures. One was of his mansion, all taped off and there was a big white forensic tent erected. There a picture of each of the victims including Carrie, wearing exactly the same pinafore she wore every time I saw her, there was also a picture of his office which police had apparently searched thoroughly. It looked creepy and barren. I bookmarked the important articles and pictures with slips of paper then took everything through to the living room, scanned the pictures on our computer and printed them out.

"Hi sweetheart," Granda said appearing by my side with a pop. I didn't even jump.

"Hi, where's Carrie?"

"She's gone for a quick visit to see her nieces."

"Nieces?"

"Yes she had nine brothers and sisters and they are all in their sixties and seventies now. They all have children and even grandchildren now. I think it was something she wanted to do alone."

"Wow I didn't even think that she might have family still alive."

"Quite a lot of family actually, spread all over Scotland. How's the research going?"

"Well I've just printed out the stuff I think might be of some use. I got some definite dates. I think tomorrow perhaps you and Carrie should have a poke around his house just in case. It's a mega long shot but there might be something in the attic or you might be able to see under floorboards or something."

"You thought this through honey. I'm really proud of you."

"Well its worth doing it just to rule it out. On Thursday I'm going to look at this microfilm thingy, that ought to fry my brain."

"You've got a good head on your shoulder quine, like your ma."

"Thanks Granda."

"I love you Petal."

"Aw Granda love you too."

A yawn escaped my lips. I glanced at the clock. It was only eight 'o' clock and I still had my regular homework to do. I gathered all the articles and went back through to my bedroom and put them all away in a clear A4 wallet. Lucky the homework was pretty light and I finished quickly while Granda hovered over me asking about my day. Just after nine I heard the front door to the building slam and then a few seconds later mum came through the flat door.

"I've got Chinese Roxy, come and get it."

"Cool mum, be right there."

Carrie appeared.

"I can't stay," she said. "I have to go back to the school now."

Granda who was sat on my bed, stood up.

"Let's go then little one," he said clapping his hands together. Carrie smiled warmly and they both vanished after saying their goodbyes. Yum, I could smell the takeaway wafting through and the chocolate cake seemed hours ago. I put away my completed homework and went through to the kitchen.

"You OK Roxy, how was your day?"

"It's was really good mum."

"And who's this boy, Brandon?" she said mischievously.

"Just a boy mum. Our maths teacher asked me to help him with his algebra."

"And?"

"That's it mum, he has a girlfriend."

I loaded my plate with sweet and sour king prawn, my favourite.

"How's nana doing?" I said taking a seat at the dining table.

"She's doing good, coping really well. But I'm going to go over as much as I can after work and weekends. Is that OK love?"

"Of course it is."

"What about you Roxy? You seem to be coping the best out of all of us."

"I'm good mum, just trying to keep myself busy."

"I know it's hard to believe he's gone."

"I know mum." I put my fork down, reached out and touched mum's hand. I had been so pre-occupied with Granda returning and Carrie appearing that I had forgotten that those close to me were mourning the loss of Granda. I realised my mum was coping remarkably well. We had always been so tight-knit as a family and mum was more like a friend than a mother. We hung out together at home, watched movies and did each other's nails. She was a great mum and I loved her lots.

"Is there anything I can do to help?" I offered.

"You are helping Rox."

"How?" I said, puzzled.

"Because you enable me to take care of Nana when she needs it the most. I can leave you and trust that you'll do your homework and not throw parties in the flat. You have done your homework?"

"Yes mum."

"See there you go. You're a good girl Rox and that's all I need right now. You want to watch a DVD?"

We plonked ourselves on the sofa, our tummies bursting with takeaway and snuggled up. Mum played idly away with my hair while we watched *Mama Mia* and sang along. Mum adored Abba and we'd been to the cinema twice to see that movie. Mum came once with me, Annabel and Jennifer but none of us minded, she was a super-trendy mum. When the credits started rolling it was just after eleven. I gave mum a kiss on the cheek, yawned, yawned some more then went through to bed and I was asleep as soon as my PJs were on.

Chapter 8

"You were supposed to call me," Annabel exclaimed when we all met up for school the next day.

"I'm sorry, me and mum spent the evening together, you know, she was a bit upset."

"Oh, I'm sorry."

"No it's fine, I'm sorry I forgot."

"So come on, dish the gossip."

I delighted in telling them about the previous evening. The cake, the hot chocolate and the lovely warning I had gotten from Tiffany.

"The cow," Jennifer said.

"I know. I'm not going to be intimidated by her though," I replied.

"Too right, someone should put a curse on her. Do you think he likes you? Be honest?" Annabel asked.

"Don't be daft. You have seen him haven't you?"

"Hey don't put yourself down like that."

"I'm not but he is way out of my league. I'm just being a realist."

"Well I think you might be surprised Rox," Jennifer said

sincerely. "Come on, we got maths first thing this morning so let's see how much tutoring actually went on."

I gave her a swift dig in the ribs in return.

Brandon entered maths after I had taken my seat. Tiffany was with him. I could never understand why the hell she was in advanced maths in the first place. I consoled myself with the fact that she always seemed to be at the bottom, asking anyone who would take her on the answers. I never accommodated her. She had been a thorn in my side since the start of school. She had rich snobby parents and even had a flaming Gucci purse… at school for crying out loud! She was one of those girls that was popular for all the wrong reasons. She smoked, bunked off school and I'd even heard girls in the toilets saying she'd been going to parties and getting really drunk but she still had a steady following of mini Tiffany's at her ankles. I just didn't get it.

Anyway Brandon gave me a wave and a thank you as he passed, then Tiffany yanked on his arm and he took his seat behind me. Mr Winters arrived shortly after and we all got out our text books.

"OK people, Pythagoras' Theorem. You've covered the basics now it's time for more depth, more structure."

There were a few moans and groans.

"Page fifty-six people. Come on maths is fun, fun, fun," his voice full of humour.

I looked up as he spoke and was mortified to see Carrie walk through the door and approach my desk. Jennifer glanced at me to and I quickly hid my expression of dread and put my head back down.

"I'm really sorry Roxy but you need to come with me."

I looked up at her and gave her THE look.

"I wouldn't ask if it wasn't important."

I rolled my eyes and raised my hand.

"Yes Roxanne?" Mr Winters asked.

"Can I please go to the bathroom?"

"Of course."

I left the class and as soon as the door shut behind me I turned to Carrie.

"It better be important, it better be life or death."

I followed her up the corridor and into the toilet where I had encountered the essence. I cringed slightly because I hadn't actually used that toilet since, even though it was a huge detour to the next nearest one.

Granda was waiting for us.

"You guys can't do this," I moaned "I need to live a normal life you can't just puff into my maths class willy nilly."

As I was giving my mini-lecture, Carrie had put her hand through the toilet cubicle wall and was slowly retracting it. She stopped as if she were trying to pull something out that didn't want to come.

"It's OK," she whispered softly. "Roxanne is our friend."

Holding Carrie's hand was a smaller hand and then out stepped a little girl.

"You are kidding?" I said.

I didn't mean to sound harsh but I had enough on my plate with all that had happened. The little girl was undeniably cute and adorable. She had jet black hair tied into two bunches with pink ribbon. She was wearing very old-fashioned looking clothes and she looked to me to be about five years old.

"I need my bear," she said quietly, her voice was barely audible.

"What's the matter honey?" I asked.

"My bear, I need to find my bear. I lost him, see."

I turned to face Carrie who was wincing slightly.

"Listen, pulling me out of class because you've been murdered and the headmaster has stashed your body somewhere in the school THAT would have been a valid reason. Pulling me out of class because some kid has lost her bear that's just…"

"Roxanne May McDonald," Granda shouted. I jumped nearly six feet in the air with shock; Granda almost never shouted at me. "I thought your mother had raised you better. Look at this little girl, she's been wandering around Aberdeen for over a hundred years and you can help her."

OK that made me feel really crappy and I hung my head slightly.

"I'm sorry Granda. OK how do I help?"

"That's better. Now it's simple we have to go and get her bear and take it to her."

"OK that does sound simple. Where's the bear?"

"Stonehaven."

"Ok that's do-able. Where about?"

"Erm, the Tollbooth Museum," Granda said quickly.

"A museum?"

"Yes but its not guarded or anything."

"So you want me to steal it!"

Now Granda was looking very shifty. He spent a few seconds examining his feet and lifting the front of his slippers with his toes.

"Well it's not stealing is it, I mean it belongs to her," Carrie interjected.

"Quiet you. Right let's recap. So you want me to skip school, grab a bus to Stonehaven which is like thirty miles away. Once there you want me to steal a priceless bear from a museum, correct."

"Yes" they said together.

"Right so once I have it she'll disappear."

"Well no," Carrie said.

"So what do I do if I get it?"

"Well we've been talking to little Amy here to see what she needs to pass over, haven't we petal?"

The little girl nodded.

"Well once you have the bear you take it to her."

"But she can come with us can't she."

"Yes but you have to take the bear TO her." "What to her body?" I was going to have a panic attack.

"She's buried in St Machar's," Granda added.

"What so I just put the bear on her grave?"

"Well no, you'll have to bury it with her." Granda saw the sheer terror on my face. "You won't have to dig all the way down just enough so that no-one will dig it up or steal it."

Then suddenly I was slightly angry at being made to feel horrible.

"Granda, you lecture me about being brought up properly then ask me to bunk off school, rob a museum then dig up a little girl's grave. All in one afternoon."

"Well no, you'll have to dig the grave at night." Granda smiled sheepishly.

Carrie was trying to keep a straight face.

"No way."

"Graveyards are the safest places to be," Carrie said.

"Yes, says the ghost."

"We know it's a lot to ask. But that's what has to be done for her to pass over," Granda said.

"Well why didn't you pass over?"

"I'm not sure," he answered, perplexed by the sudden change of subject. "I think I'm to see that you're happy."

"Me, why?"

"That's all me and your nana have ever wanted."

"Aww Granda." I felt my resolve weakening.

I couldn't quite believe what I was doing as I made my way back to class. I approached Mr Winters at his desk. Carrie had followed behind me and Granda waited in the hall with Amy.

70

"Erm, Mr Winters." I tried to look unwell. "I'm not feeling too good, would it be OK if I went home?" He surprisingly understood and gave me the homework he was going to hand out after class.

"You do look a bit peaky Roxanne. Make sure you rest OK?" He looked really concerned which made me feel even guiltier. I made my way back out to the corridor where Granda was waiting patiently. I have to admit I was in a really bad mood. I hated missing school so much that I once even dragged myself in with food poisoning. I caught the bus on Holburn Street, off the main road near our school. Luckily I had a little money on me for my fare there and back. I took a seat near the back and Granda, Carrie and Amy sat in front of me. I didn't feel like speaking so I sat and looked out of the window. To keep Amy amused Granda started singing the *Wheels on the Bus* Carrie soon joined in and it got louder and louder and only I could hear it. Fabulous, just fabulous.

After the wheels went round and the horn went beep, and the ladies went chatter and other seemingly endless verses, we pulled into the little fishing village called Stonehaven. The Tollbooth Museum was the oldest building in the village. Upstairs there was a famous fish restaurant and downstairs was the museum itself. My three ghostly companions had been right, once inside the place was completely unguarded which made me feel totally horrid. The teddy bear in question was located at the back of a display showing you how cotton was weaved.

"Go and keep guard," I hissed at Granda.

I looked around nervously expecting a security guard to pounce on me. Suddenly I grabbed the bear and stuffed it into my bag. I hung around for a little while not wanting anyone to question why I had only stayed five minutes, I even got out my note pad and made a few fake notes. My cover story if questioned would have been I was I was doing some research for a history project. When I felt I'd browsed enough, I made my way back out and as I passed the reception there were several tourist brochures and a donation box. I'd got a return ticket for the bus so I put all the money from my purse in the box, it was only about seven pounds but I wanted to make some amends. One of the museum workers was sweeping the front path outside as I left and I gave her my warmest smile and was relieved I didn't look guilty enough to warrant a bag search. The fresh air and the enormity of what I had done hit me and I hurried to the bus stop feeling slightly sick. I actually almost felt like crying, so it was good I was the only one there. I'd never so much as nicked one of those blue pens from Argos. I hoped if there was a God, and this was the only way for one of the stray sheep from his flock to return to him, then I was hoping he would overlook my minor piece of law-breaking. Finally my heart rate slowly decreased as I realised I'd done it and hadn't been caught. But that was the easy bit compared to what I had to do next.

I heard a pop, pop, pop and my three accomplices appeared.

"Did you get it poppet?"

"Yes Granda, Project Grand Theft is complete, on with Project Grave Dig. I don't know what I'm gonna tell mum."

"Tell her you're studying at a friend's."

"Hmm, nice Granda. I'll add lying to my list of crimes for the day?" I said rather sharply.

"Now, now. No need to be shirty young lady. "

"Humph." I folded my hands over my chest in a very unlady-like fashion. I knew I was being a brat but I'd never stolen anything in my life and I was feeling mighty guilty.

I kept expecting the bus to be pulled over all the way home. I shifted nervously in my seat. Granda seemed to know why I was so sullen and he tried to reassure me I was doing the right thing by Amy. I was relieved when we got back home and the flat was empty. I hid the teddy bear in the back of my wardrobe, grabbed a can of drink out of the fridge and started to make my way back out.

"Where are you going?" Granda asked.

"There's no point in me hanging around here is there and I can't do anything about the bear just now. I'm gonna go apologise to Mr Winters and see what I missed. I'll just say I feel better. Then I'll go to the bank after school and draw some money out so I can get a taxi tonight."

"Well you seem to have it all planned out Roxy, you're so clever," Carrie added.

"Don't try to sweet talk me you evil entity."

Little Amy who was holding Granda's hand chuckled.

Help my Granda is Haunting Me!

"You lot are just going to hang around me until I'm committed aren't you?"

Chapter 9

I found Mr Winters sat at his desk. It was just coming up to the start of afternoon classes. He smiled warmly when he saw me.

"Ah Roxanne, hello."

"I had a lie down for an hour sir and I feel a bit better. I'm sorry I missed class."

"Don't be sorry it shows commitment that you've come back. You'll be pleased to know there was a marked improvement in Brandon's work."

"Fantastic."

"You didn't miss very much. We did a few mock questions at the end of the lesson, nothing you can't handle." He handed me the work he had given out to the rest of the class. "Have a look over those and do the homework I gave you earlier so you are up to speed, OK? Now then, I'll let you get to your next lesson."

"OK, thanks again Mr Winters."

"No problem."

I headed for the door.

"Oh and Roxanne?"

"Yes sir."

"Is everything else alright?"

I assumed he was talking about losing Granda.

"I'm doing OK."

"That's good, I'm here if you need any help. Or just someone to talk to, a friendly ear."

"Thank you sir."

He gave me a genuine smile and his head went down to carry on marking. What a nice guy.

I texted Annabel and she told me her and Jen were in the library just about to go to class. We didn't have class together that afternoon but I was nearby so I met them and filled them in on my illness. I told them I suspected it was period cramp. I really hated telling lies, especially to my two best friends but what choice did I have? If I told them I'd bunked off school to help the ghost of a small child I'd have been committed. We headed for the toilet to freshen up before we went to afternoon registration then onto class.

"You fancy coming over to mine tonight you two?" Jennifer asked.

"Actually that's a great idea," I replied. "Count me in."

That would work out great because then I wouldn't really be lying to mum, I'd just be making a slight detour to do a bit of digging.

"*I'm not going if she's going.*" Jennifer and I both looked at Annabel, startled. The voice came from her mouth but it was altered and distorted. I looked in horror as her eyes rolled into the back of her head until just the whites of her eyeballs showed and then a wicked, evil smile appeared on her face.

"Annabel?" Jennifer said nervously.

"Ditching your friends at the first opportunity." Her head snapped from side to side, twitching, moving fast then coming to stop only to start twitching again a few seconds later. I nearly pooped in my drawers.

"We need to get help." I shouted.

"No, you'd better get some help." Now Jennifer's voice had changed too and so had her eyes. They both took slow steps towards me and I backed away until I was at the far wall of the bathroom. Both their heads twitched violently from side to side and their eyes blazed white. Their laughter rang out, their voices high pitched and distorted.

"Snap out of it you two," I cried out desperately. Nothing. They both carried on approaching me. I grabbed a small waste paper basket made of woven metal and threw in their general direction. It missed but the bottom of bin hit the mirror, it didn't smash but the noise was deafening.

They both dropped to the floor and a thin trail of blood ran out of their noses. I ran over to them. They were both breathing but they were unconscious. I shook them in turns to try to waken them.

Annabel came round first.

"What happened?" she said groggily.

"I dunno you two just dropped like flies, it's so hot in here."

"You think it was the heat?"

"I don't know, how do you feel?"

"A bit disorientated."

I tried to calm down quickly. I knew full well it had been Mr Ratchet behind their behaviour. I reached into my bag, removed a bottle of water and some tissue, and handed them to Annabel. As she took a gulp, Jennifer started to come round too.

"Are you OK Jen?" I asked.

"I think so, what happened?"

"You and Annabel passed out. I think it might have been the heat."

"Did you?"

"No but I felt dizzy. Maybe we should go see the nurse," I suggested.

"I feel OK now," Jennifer said.

"Me too," Annabel added. "Weird, huh?"

They decided they would go if they felt dizzy again and I was immensely relieved. We went to registration and then I headed off on my own to my afternoon classes agreeing to meet up after school. I was a bag of nerves as I walked down the corridors. I looked at everyone's eyes and I kept glancing over my shoulder. I had absolutely no idea what I was up against. This wasn't some two bit ghost from a *Scooby-doo* episode; I was nearly killed, and by my two best friends too. I drifted through my afternoon classes by the skin of my teeth. I jumped every time anyone spoke to me and I couldn't concentrate on a thing the teachers said. Not like me at all.

I had never been so glad to hear the bell for the end of the school day and for the first time, like ever, I didn't want to go back the next day. I wanted to stay as far away from Mr Ratchet as I possibly could.

I met Jennifer and Annabel as we'd agreed and we made plans to go to Jennifer's at eight that evening. I stopped by a cash point and drew out some money for a taxi. The toilet incident wasn't mentioned, out of embarrassment I presumed. I kept quiet, I was still in shock. When we parted ways and I entered the flat I was relieved to be home. Mum was at nana's so I grabbed a sausage roll and went into my bedroom where I could hear the three stooges laughing about something. I opened the door not quite sure what I was going to find.

Granda was on all fours on my bedroom floor and Amy was riding him round like a horse. Carrie watched on in amusement from the bed.

"Hi guys," I greeted.

"Hi," was the hearty reply from them all.

"I need to tell you something."

They stopped the horseplay and gave me their full attention. I filled them in on the toilet incident.

"He must know that you are helping me," Carrie said looking worried.

"I know you said he had the ability to transmit ill-feeling but flaming heck, I was really scared. I thought they were gonna kill me, they were all twitchy and icky."

"I'm sorry."

"Hey, it's not your fault, but what happens if we do free you? I mean, won't that mean he'll have a free rein."

"No, because I'm the last evil deed, if I pass he will too."

"Ah, right. Well look it's getting dark, I'm going to order a taxi and stick mum a note on the fridge. Are you coming with me?"

"Of course we are. Amy's been so excited all day," Granda said. "Haven't you petal?" The little girl nodded enthusiastically.

I wrote a note saying I was going to be at Jennifer's if she needed me. It wasn't a lie, not really. I would be there eventually, I was just taking a small detour to the cemetery to dig up a small child's grave; just your average night really.

The taxi was prompt and the traffic was at a minimum, thank God. The graveyard in question was in the old part of Aberdeen near the university. I was a total bag of nerves. I paid the ridiculous fare and slung my bag over my shoulder (complete with grave digging equipment). The taxi driver sped off and within seconds the three ghosts pop, pop, popped in front of me. That was definitely a handy trick. I stared down the street leading to the cemetery. It was dark, eerie and dimly lit. I shivered.

"So will there be any ghosts here?" I asked.

"Very unlikely," Carrie said.

"I wonder why?"

"Well most ghosts feel compelled to hang around the thing that is needed to make them pass over. I hang around the school because that's where I'm buried, Granda hangs around you because he wants to see you happy and little Amy, well she spent most of her time in the museum but we found her wandering around opposite your school, that's where she used to live. The point is that most ghosts do not need to hang around their bodies, there's no reason to."

"Gotcha, still don't feel very safe though. Do you even know where her grave is?"

"Aye, we've been today and found it," Granda said proudly.

"You're like my three dead sidekicks. Seriously though, no more ghosts until we have sorted out Carrie. I don't care how cute they are."

We walked down the cobbled street. The houses on the left were huge and overbearing and only a couple of lights could be seen glowing through the thick curtains. I walked as fast as I could - so wanting it over with. The cemetery looked spooky in the moonlight. I got a torch out from my grave digging bag and followed the ghosts deep inside. We passed headstone after headstone until we reached an older part of the cemetery and I finally saw Amy's grave. I was glad they had located it during the day because it was a tiny little stone in comparison with those surrounding it.

Here lies Amy Dodsworth
Dearly missed
1895-1899
Find peace in the arms of God

"That's so sad," I said.

"Come on Roxy honey, let's not hang about," Granda replied.

He was right of course, it wasn't the sort of place I wanted to spend any time in unnecessarily. I pulled my mum's small gardening trowel out of my bag and Granda gave me a funny look.

"Hey we don't have a garden so this was the best I could do and besides I could hardly get a taxi to a graveyard carrying a big shovel could I?"

"True," he chuckled.

I got down on my knees and with the trowel I skimmed a circle of grass about a foot in diameter, wide enough for the bear. I then started to dig up the dirt while I wondered idly how deep they put the bodies in. When the hole was a foot and a half deep I figured that was about as deep as I felt comfortable going. I got the bear out of my bag and placed it at the bottom of the hole. I replaced all the dirt, stamped it flat with my feet then replaced the circle of grass and stamped on that too. It didn't look like it had been disturbed.

We all turned to look at Amy. At first she didn't look any different and I thought, I was going to have to put the flaming bear in deeper, but then her face broke into a huge smile and the brightest light you've ever seen escaped from the end of her fingertips. She brought them up to her face, looking at them in wonder, then she looked over to me. As I watched in amazement the bright light was now coming out of her shoes and it cast bright beams across the graveyard. It was like staring into the sun but so beautiful you couldn't look away. The light travelled up her arms and legs, getting brighter and brighter, it consumed her body until just her shoulders and head remained.

"Thank you," she said brightly.

The light covered her face and I brought my arm up to shield my eyes. Then it caved in on itself and in seconds she had disappeared. The darkness surrounding us seemed darker still.

"Wow," I said in complete awe.

"Well done honey," Granda said.

I hadn't felt this good... well ever. Something within me felt elated, taken to a higher plane. My mind had totally opened up in those few minutes and now it yearned to help more stray ghosts pass over.

"That was... wow. So she's really gone?"

"Yup," Carrie replied.

"Great, well the university is back up on the main road, the café bit should still be open, so I guess we'd better head out. I'm gonna get a hot chocolate and call a cab."

"I need to get back to school."

"OK, well you two go. I have access to the microfilm tomorrow so hopefully we'll find something out."

"You did really good Roxy," Carrie said.

"Thanks, it felt really good."

The two ghosts smiled at me.

Help my Granda is Haunting Me!

"Come on, we'll make sure you get to the top of the street and then we'll get gone," Granda said.

At the top of the road to the cemetery there was a large university campus and on the main road was a café that was open to the public. I phoned a taxi from my mobile and asked them to alert me when they were outside, then I ordered a hot chocolate and took a seat. All the students were studying or socialising, and I hoped that someday I would be attending somewhere like this, although I wasn't overly sure what I wanted to do. I was quite good at anything I applied myself to. I sometimes thought I enjoyed maths so much I'd like to teach it but I wasn't sure I could cope with teenagers like some of the more rowdy ones in our school.

Jennifer had never really been interested in making anything of herself. Her mum and dad were traditionalists and Jennifer was looking forward to settling down, getting married, having children and making her husband happy. No matter how hard I tried I couldn't picture myself as a wife and mother. While I didn't agree with Jennifer's career choice one bit, as a good friend I would support her all the way, minus dirty nappies, yuck! Annabel on the other hand was determined to go to university to study art. She worked part-time at the weekend and was already squirrelling money away to fund her education. Annabel was a true artist in every way, she carried an artist's pad with her and she was interested in tarot cards and stuff like that. She could be found most weekends in Merlin's Grove, a magical supply shop where she bought incense and a whole load of other stuff I couldn't get my head around. Most of it didn't logically make sense to me. Mind you with recent events I was beginning to believe that anything could be out there. My mobile phone rang in my pocket, it was the taxi driver. I popped the lid on my hot chocolate, made my way outside and hopped in.

It didn't take long to get to Jennifer's house and when I looked at my watch I saw the whole grave digging mission had only taken thirty-five minutes.

Jen's mum answered the door warmly.

"Come in Roxanne sweetheart. I baked cookies for you girls."

"Thank you."

Annabel and Jennifer were waiting in Jennifer's bedroom, they were doing homework.

"Hi guys."

"Hi," they replied.

Jennifer pulled a fluffy cushion from her bed and put it on the floor for me to join them. I threw my bag to the side and plonked myself down cross-legged.

"How you feeling Roxy?" Jennifer asked.

"I'm feeling good. How about you two, you feeling better?"

"Better? I never felt ill."

I thought quick and covered my tracks because obviously they had no recollection of the toilet incident.

"I got you mixed up with someone else, sorry. Hey can I jump on your computer, check Facebook?"

"Sure some of us have normal-sized brains that take a little longer to absorb schoolwork before we can do fun stuff," Jennifer grinned.

"I can give you guy's a hand just gimmie a shout."

"Too right we will, what's the point in having a smart friend if she won't help you," Annabel laughed.

I jumped up, clicked on the computer and sat at the office-type chair.

Jennifer was really lucky to have a computer in her room. Her parents weren't much interested in stuff like that. Her dad was football mad, (Aberdeen of course) and her mum never really got on the whole internet bandwagon. I logged into my favourite social networking site, Facebook. I hadn't had chance to get on it since Granda had died and I was sure all my crops had withered and died by now on Farmville.

I noticed I had a friend request. I clicked to see who it was. Brandon!

"Oh my God, you guys! Brandon sent me a friend request."

"No way," they both chorused. Homework was suddenly forgotten and both girls jumped up and crowded the computer.

"Come on Rox, accept already!" Jennifer squealed.

With a shaky hand I clicked on accept.

"It's probably just to talk about math's stuff, I mean let's be realistic," I said.

"Hey, don't put yourself down like that," Jennifer replied.

"I'm not. I know I'm not ugly but girls like me don't get boys like him."

"Your being sensible Rox. It's good, I don't want to see you get hurt," Annabel added.

Brandon wasn't online so Jen and Annabel returned to the floor where they became engrossed in their homework once more.

I loaded up Farmville and began harvesting my bell peppers and collecting fruit. Some really nice friend had watered my crops in my absence so they were all ripe for the picking. Suddenly a little chat bubble popped up in the corner of the screen. It was Brandon.

"Hi," it said simply.

I fought the urge to tell my friends. I just wanted it to be a private moment even if it was one of friendship and nothing more.

"Hi," I typed back.

"Missed you in maths. You feeling OK?"

"Yes was just a little sick but OK now. How did you find Pi?"

"Definitely easier thanks to you."

"No probs. Friday we can just stick to the library."

"Yes cool. Well I'd better go, my dinner is here. Got Indian takeaway. Maybe see you tomorrow. Bye x."

"Bye x."

Did it mean anything that he had put a kiss at the end I asked myself? I knew it didn't though, I put a kiss after every text I sent to Annabel and Jennifer, it meant nothing. I ignored the flutter of hope in my stomach, logged off the computer and sat down on the rug and helped Annabel and Jennifer with their science homework. We ate home baked cookies until I felt sick and at nine thirty Jennifer's mum offered to drop me and Annabel off at home.

When I arrived back to my flat Mum was watching some soaps she had recorded on Sky plus.

"You want a cup of tea mum?" I offered.

"Yes please honey. How was your day?"

"Not bad, how's nana holding up?"

"She seemed OK today. She was talking about Granda. She'll have her good and bad days."

I made tea and popped some biscuits on a side dish and took a seat on the sofa next to mum. I drank my tea and snuggled in. I hated soaps but mum and nana absolutely loved them. I was content to watch them because mum started playing with my hair and it was soothing. I felt my eyes growing heavy and I think I drifted off a couple of times. At eleven I kissed mum goodnight brushed my teeth and put my jammies on.

What a really good, weird and wonderful day, I thought to myself. I had committed some crimes I wouldn't be sharing with anyone anytime soon, but it had all become worth it when I had freed Amy. That had been a great feeling and it made me think that as I'd been given this wonderful gift that I should accept it and help these poor souls that were trapped and eager to move on. I had Granda too, he could round up the stray ghosts and keep them occupied so that on the surface I could lead the normal life of a teenager, well normal for me. I just hoped that I could do the same for Carrie.

Then there was my new virtual friendship with Brandon. OK so the conversation had been really short and Brandon had always been really friendly anyway, but I felt that it had been more than that. I wanted to push these feelings down to the pit of my stomach but I had really got the impression that Brandon had flirted with me in Starbucks. That was silly and stupid. He went out with girls like Britney and Tiffany and if he wasn't dating anyone then there was literally a stream of pretty girls following him around waiting to be the next arm candy.

Chapter 10

The next day I told myself I wasn't looking around every corner trying to catch a glimpse of him. It was just so unfair. I totally didn't want my brain incapacitated by thoughts of him but I couldn't help it. To make matters even worse someone had stuck up posters everywhere about a Halloween ball. I never went to those things, mainly because I'd never had anyone to take me but also because I didn't need to. They were stupid and unnecessary... honest!

Tiffany on the other hand was proudly telling everyone how she was going to buy THE most expensive dress and she might even borrow some of her mother's diamonds. If she spoke any louder she would be screeching and I got the feeling her little performance was for me. Someone should have handed her a megaphone then she could have held it a foot from my ear, that would have been more subtle. I was glad when the teacher came into the history lesson and she shut the hell up.

I pictured what it would be like going to the ball. I saw myself wearing a dressy dress and heels perhaps. I owned two pairs of heels and I'd never had the occasion to wear them. I could imagine the dancing, laughing and being on the arm of a gorgeous boy like Tiffany would be. Oh my God, I was jealous of Tiffany, suddenly I was depressed.

"Roxanne?"

The voice evaporated my daydream and I frowned in annoyance.

"Roxanne, seeing as you know everything there is to know about farming perhaps you would like to tell the rest of the class the difference between sedentary and nomadic."

The history teacher had a smirk on his face that said he just knew I wouldn't know the answer.

"Sedentary is where the farmer is based in the same location and nomadic is where the farmer moves from place to place."

"Humph… well, stop daydreaming and pay attention." Annabel who sat next to me in geography started giggling but stopped abruptly when the teacher shot her a look that said 'the next person to cross me will pay'.

At the end of the day I headed for the library to use the microfilm. The same librarian was behind the desk. Today she had on a really nice trouser suit and square designer glasses. She recognised me and smiled warmly.

"Hello there, I have all the dates looked out for you. There's quite an amount to get through."

"That's OK. I'll have a look until you close up and come back another day if I need to."

"Come on though and I'll show you how it works."

I'd never been through the back and was surprised to find quite a large room which housed all the school archives.

Against one wall were rows and rows of chunky open wooden shelves filled with box files. There were several desks set up in the centre of the room and then off to one side was a huge copy machine and the infamous microfilm.

"OK," the librarian began. "I've already put the disc in for you and I've set it to the last date you requested so you can scroll back from there. Now it's hooked up to the computer and printer at the desk so if there's anything you need to print then you hit this button, here, and you can collect it later on your way out."

"Sounds good," I replied. She turned, disappeared back through the front leaving me to my task. I wished Granda and Carrie had materialised, two more sets of eyes scanning the hundreds of articles would have been handy but I'd told them to nip and see Nana. After about fifteen minutes searching I started to come across articles about Mr Ratchet. They were the most recent so they were about him hanging himself then as I flicked back even more I picked up the stories of the girls going missing. I printed the odd article off but didn't really find anything new. Once I passed the dates of the abductions there were a few articles about how Mr Ratchet's teachings were frowned upon. It was around the time where children still received the cane at school but it seemed Mr Ratchet dished out several canings a day and really hurt some of the girls.

I started flicking through as fast as I could really only looking at the headlines. Then I came across a large picture of Mr Ratchet. It made me stop dead instantly. The article was about him being appointed Headmaster. He was sat in his office, a huge fire was merrily roaring away and he was holding a gold plaque with his name on it. Even with his wide smile he looked eerie and creepy and it gave me the heebie-jeebies just looking at him. Instantly something about the picture bothered me. I put it down to his general creepiness and hit the print button with a heavy thud to mark the end of my task at least for that day.

"You should not be here."

The librarian had appeared in the door way, her eyes rolled back and her head snapping manically from side to side. I shot up out of my seat and backed myself up until I was jammed into an aisle where the archives were.

"Meddling, meddling. Children should be seen and not heard."

I started to hyperventilate with fear. Her face was totally vacant as she made her way towards me. When she was just about two feet away she stopped, looked me square in the eye and smiled at my fear.

Thank God Carrie chose that moment to enter. She popped in just behind the librarian and gave me a wave.

"For God sake, help me!" I screamed.

Carrie cottoned on quickly. She ran towards me passing through the librarian whose head stopped jerking and a thin trickle of blood ran from her nose before she collapsed onto the floor.

"Thank God Carrie! I was so scared. How did you do that?"

"It's difficult, but because I am a pure spirit if I think positive thoughts as I pass through them it interrupts the essence's negativity."

"This is getting scary. Where's Granda?"

"We checked in on your nana, your mum was there so we decided to check out Mr Ratchet's house. I said I would come back and check on you. Granda said he would nip back to his house then meet us at your flat."

"You've been to check out Mr Ratchet's old house?"

"Yes, well it was your suggestion. We thought we'd give you a bit of space and see if we could find anything."

"And?"

"Nothing. There's a family living there now. We checked the attic but it seems like every trace has gone."

"Oh, well it was a long shot. Thanks for doing that."

"No problem."

"I'm getting out of here."

"I think I'm going to have to stay with you from now on."

"I'm not disagreeing with that."

I heaved the librarian to the side of the room and sat her up against a cupboard.

"Will she be alright?"

"Yes, they tend not to remember when they have been influenced by him."

"I know! My friends didn't remember about yesterday."

"It saves you explaining."

"I suppose."

I hurried through to the main part of the library, grabbed my print outs and got the hell out of there. When I arrived home I began to read up on some of the articles. I showed Carrie some of the ones I thought were interesting. It wasn't long before Granda appeared and he was beside himself when he found out about the library incident.

"I can't believe we left you in danger petal, I thought you'd be safe in the library with loads of people around."

"I'm fine Granda and how were you to know really. I was the one that said I would be OK."

"Maybe you should say you're ill and stay home pet."

"No, I need to be at school and besides I'll be able to research better there."

"I don't like it Roxy but if you insist we will have to stick to you like glue."

"But I should be alright in classes shouldn't I?"

"Yes," Carrie answered. "The more people are with you the safer you are. We'll see you to each class then we'll wait outside or we'll hang around school. Right well we better get back but we'll wait for you tomorrow at the entrance."

"You OK Roxy?" Granda said looking very concerned.

"Yes Granda, I think we must be close, he's getting worried."

"Just be careful."

"I will."

"Right well I'll see you in the morning."

"Big kiss Granda."

"To you too honey."
And they were gone.

Chapter 11

The next day was Friday. I didn't know whether to be ecstatic, after all Friday meant a whole hour alone with Brandon, or scared, what the heck was I going to do if Brandon went all twitchy on me. On the other hand, a whole hour with Brandon!

Another thing really playing on my mind was the niggling feeling that I was missing something with regards to my Mr Ratchet investigation. I was also really worried that I wouldn't be able to help Carrie at all. I was trying to solve a case from decades ago. What was I going to do if there was no evidence left to find? I tried to think positive but it was hard. As I approached the school arm in arm with Annabel and Jennifer, I saw Granda and Carrie waiting for me at the entrance to the school as promised. They waved and followed behind us.

'I can do this,' I said over and over again in my head.

"Rox, wait up." My heart did a funny little somersault as I heard Brandon's voice. He was just getting out of the huge 4x4. We all stopped and waited for him to catch us up. He wasn't even out of breath when he reached us.

"I just wanted to check if we were still meeting in the library."

"Yes sure." I remained calm and aloof, I think. "Cool. Well I'd better go. I'll see you there."

"Sure, I catch you later."

I watched him walk away and then my arm was yanked as Annabel brought me back to reality.

"I really think he likes you," Jennifer cooed.

"Do we have to go through this again? He is just nice in general, he's like that with everyone."

Jennifer shook her head in a really annoying smug and knowing way, and I jabbed her playfully with my elbow.

True to their word my two heavenly guardians were glued to my side all morning. I learned quickly to ignore Granda's hilarious comments about the latest fashions and remain straight faced. He had difficulty understanding leg warmers to the point where I actually nearly turned round to tell him to pipe down.

They left me alone in my classes which enabled me to concentrate. Straight after lunch was the study period so I made my way to the library. I realised instantly that it was a bad idea. It looked like everyone who had the hour free was in the library including Tiffany. I had serious doubts as to whether she could actually read so I had no idea why she was in the library. I took a seat near the back where it was quieter and got out *Blood and Granite* to do a bit of research. I'd barely read a paragraph before the dumping of a bag on the table in front of me made me jump out of my skin.

"Sorry," Brandon said. He didn't look sorry as he smiled cheekily at me.

"No problem," I laughed. "I guess I was a little absorbed."

"What you reading?"

"It's for a history project," I said showing him the book.

"Cool, so what do you want to do today?"

"Hmm, let's see."

Tiffany chose that very moment to bound over, hair flopping everywhere and planted a big kiss on Brandon's cheek.

"Hey baby, watcha doing." I hated her voice soooooo much.

"I told you Tiff, I've really got to get this studying done."

"OK honey buns." She winked at me and rejoined her group of clingons in the corner. They weren't even attempting to study or read, and seemed content to gossip and snigger.

Brandon gave me an apologetic look and rummaged in his bag bringing out his work from the previous maths lesson. He'd improved heaps.

"You really got the hang of it Brandon, you probably don't need me you know," I said being honest.

"Oh, it's a bit much to ask of you isn't it? I know you must have way better things to do than coaching maths."

"No, no. It's not that. I honestly don't mind but I'm sure you have things you'd rather be doing."

"There's gonna be other stuff that comes up in maths. If you're OK with it then I'd like to continue. It can't hurt, can it?"

"Not at all." I tried not to smile too wide. "Give me a minute I'll jot down a few questions for you."

As I wrote down a few equations Tiffany came up behind Brandon once more and slid her arms around his neck. Brandon rolled his eyes slightly.

"Tiff, please?"

"Oh come on babes. Maths is soooooo boring. Only geeks and nerds enjoy it."

I blushed at the insult so obviously directed at me.

"I asked you heaps of times today to leave me be, I need to study this."

"I can think of better things to be doing than hanging about with frizz ball nerds who don't know their place."

"That's out of order Tiffany."

"Yes, but it's true."

"Go away." His voice deepened a tone.

"I was just joking. Geez baby."

"For Christ's sake go away will ya," he raised his voice a notch and a few people nearby turned their heads to look. Tiffany turned a deep shade of red but regained her composure quick as a flash.

"OK baby I'll catch you in a wee while."

She returned to sit with her friends but kept her heavily-lined eyes on me.

"I'm sorry about that," Brandon said.

"What do you see in her?" I asked boldly.

"At the moment, not a lot," he replied sadly.

"Sorry it's just I've had to put up with three years of Tiffany."

"We've been on and off since school started and I honestly question why I keep going back. I don't know why she has to be so nasty and jealous. She's totally different when we're alone."

"Don't sweat it, let's get some work done, eh?" I definitely didn't want to think about them alone together.

"Ok miss." He smiled.

I couldn't have been more relieved when I dumped my bag on my bed at the end of the school day. What a week! I couldn't believe how much had happened in five short days. My life had totally been turned upside down but it was worth it to have my Granda with me. I was pretty sure Tiffany hated me now instead of a mild dislike and indifference. I wasn't sure which I was more scared of; her or the evil essence of Mr Ratchet. I dismissed it as soon as I thought it, after all bullies like Tiffany crumbled when there was no one around to big them up. Granda and Carrie appeared shortly after six, I'd finished my homework and I was browsing through my Mr Ratchet research folder.

"How was today?" Granda asked. "Did we do OK?"

"You guys did great," I said genuinely. "I felt pretty relaxed by the afternoon."

"What about the investigation?"

"There's something I'm missing, I know it. It's really bugging me."

It was true I'd been looking over all the articles and something was there, I just wasn't seeing it.

"You'll get there Roxy," Carrie said. "Don't rush it. I mean I've been waiting all this time."

"I know but the essence is getting worse."

"We'll handle it. As long as I am near you I will be able to spot his influence really quickly and the more people there are around you, the harder it is for him."

"Carrie's right honey, it's great that you are helping us ghosties but we don't want you to give up your life."

"I know. Have you been to visit nana? I thought I would take the bus out to see her over the weekend."

"That's a lovely idea. I pop in and sit with her every night. She cries a lot when she is on her own but she is made of strong stuff. She'll get there and I'll be here waiting for her however long."

"Aww Granda." I felt my eyes welling up.

The next day I got up early, dressed and popped my head into mum's bedroom.

"I'm gonna go visit nana, mum."

My mum looked up, groggy from being wakened.

"If you give me half an hour I'll drive us out."

"You have a lie-in mum, I'll grab the bus. You deserve a rest."

"You sure honey, it's no trouble?"

"I'm sure. I'll see you this afternoon when I get back."

"OK sweetie."

"Love you mum."

"You too baby."

I pulled on my heavy wool coat because it was grey and it looked like it was going to rain; you've got to love Aberdeen. I made my way up on the main road, Union Street, and after glancing at the timetable was pleased to see I didn't have long to wait. I always enjoyed the ride out to my grandparents. I liked spotting bunnies and pheasants. Their house was just lovely. Granda had been so proud when they'd retired here. As their cottage came into view I lovingly remembered the trees he'd planted as little saplings that were now huge things towering over the house itself. The bus dropped me off a few houses away and it only took me a minute to reach their front door. I knocked and entered to find nana sitting in Granda's rocking chair. She smiled widely when she saw me, stood up and gave me a warm hug.

"Oh Roxy, what a lovely surprise."

"Hi nana."

I glanced around and saw that everything was exactly the same as the last time I had been here. Granda's reading glasses were resting neatly on an open novel he had been reading.

Nana saw me looking.

"I can't bear to move anything. Not just yet," she said softly.

"You don't have to nana, do it in your own time."
"I feel he's still here, especially when I'm alone. I talk to him. I'm losing it aren't I Rox?"

"Definitely not, I talk to him every day."

"Do you?"

"Yes, every day and I know he's listening to me so he must be listening to you too."

She chuckled and gave me another hug.

"Maybe we are both losing it."

"Maybe."

"Do you want some scrambled eggs?"

"Oooooo, yes please."

"Come on I'll whip up a batch with cheese."

I spent the whole day with nana and it was lovely. She dug out some home-made broth from the freezer for lunch and we ate it with bread slices as thick as doorstops. It was surprisingly easy to talk about Granda to her and it seemed to help her to chatter on about Granda's ways and mannerisms. I was so proud to see how well she was coping. I headed home in the late afternoon and the town centre was packed and busy. I said a hearty hello to an old man sitting in the bus stop and stopped in Thorntons to pick mum up her favourite chocolates. I enjoyed the walk up the main street and paused to look in some of the windows, especially Office; I adored nice shoes.

Mum had left me a wee note on the dining table saying she had gone to Asda to get a big shop in and she would be back around five. I made my way through to my bedroom and found Granda and Carrie there.

"Hey you two."

"Roxy, hi!" Carrie greeted.

"How was your day petal?" Granda added.

"Nana seems to be doing OK. She thinks she's crazy for talking to you but I set her straight."

"What did you say?" he raised an eyebrow suspiciously.

"I said I talked to you too."

"Oh aye"

"It's true, isn't it?"

"You have a fair point."

I did a few bits of homework but there wasn't really anything to do as I kept well on top of everything. The two ghosts nattered away which was strangely normal.

"I wanted to ask a small favour Roxanne if I might," Carrie said when she saw me packing away my books.

"Sure fire away."

"Well I've seen a lot of children reading a book series and I wonder if you might check one out of the library and maybe help me to read it. I won't take up a lot of your time maybe half an hour now again, I just need you to turn the pages."

"Now that's an idea," Granda exclaimed. "Can you do that for me too but I'd like to read the Evening Express."

"I don't see why not guys. What book is it Carrie?"

"*Harry Potter.*"

"Of course, every child must read *Harry Potter*. I've got the entire collection and films, I adore them. You can read them whenever you want I have them in my wardrobe."

"They are on film too?"

"Yup, next time mum is out I'll put one on in the living room and you can watch it."

Carrie looked like all her Christmases had come at once.

"Hey, that means I can watch *MASH*."

"You guys can watch what you want if mum is out. But honestly Granda did you not watch enough *MASH* when you were alive."

"The classics never get old Roxy."

I shook my head and dug out the *Philosopher's Stone* from the back of my wardrobe, laid it on my vanity table and opened it to page one. Carrie took a seat and began to read. I then went to the living room and retrieved the local newspaper, *The Evening Express*. It was a day old but I was sure Granda would appreciate it.

I laid it out on the bed and Granda sat down and began to read. I pulled my own book out, *New Moon*, got comfy on the floor and began to read. I'd been a big fan of the *Twilight* books for ages. All the girls at school were cooing over the films and everyone was either Team Edward (the lead vampire character) or Team Jacob (the lead werewolf character). When it came to the books I loved Edward but in the films I thought Jacob came off way more appealing. Jacob and Edward couldn't hold a candle to Brandon though.

Every few minutes one of the ghosts would say 'done' and I would get up and then turn the page of the book if it was Carrie or the newspaper if it was Granda. After an hour mum came back from shopping and popped her head round my door.

"Hey sweetie." She paused, looked at me reading on the floor, then at the open book on the table and then to the open newspaper on the bed.

"I'm a bit messy I'll tidy up."

"It's OK honey. How was nana?"

"Really good. I did some dusting for her."

"That was nice of you. Are you hungry?"

"Starving."

"Well give me a hand with the shopping, I bought some pizzas and garlic bread. How does that sound?"

"Cool."

Sometimes it's great living on the top floor. It was quiet, no one bothers you. The downside was when you did a huge shop. Mum frequently spent over a hundred pounds and you had to lump it all up the stairs. That particular haul was four trips each until it was all strewn on the kitchen floor.

While mum put it all away and popped the food in the oven, I gave her the chocolates I'd purchased from Thorntons.

"Here mum, I got you these."

"Aww thanks Rox, my favourite. You are a strange fifteen-year-old honey, you're supposed to cause me pain and anguish," she chuckled

"There's time yet mum," I replied cheekily.

"Don't you dare, I'm too used to the good life now."

"Can I go on the computer?"

"Sure. You want a cup of tea while we wait?"

"Can I have hot chocolate please?"

"Sure."

I clicked on the computer and waited for the old dinosaur to boot up. Granda popped his head round to announce that he and Carrie needed to head back to school. I glanced in the direction of the kitchen door, saw mum was busy and gave Granda the thumbs up.

"We'll come back in the morning sweetheart." And with a pop he was gone.

I decided I'd have a little leisure time on Facebook before pizza and then I would try to figure out what was niggling me about Carrie's case. I loaded up Farmville and was pleased to see my cotton plants were all mature and someone had kindly fertilised my crops.

"Hi there."

The little speech box popped up interrupting my hoeing. My heart skipped a beat. It was Brandon.

"Hi," I shakily typed back.

"I just wanted to say sorry again for Tiffany."

"You don't need to apologise. How are you?"

"A bit down today to be honest."

"Awww, what's up?"

"Too much to type, lol."

"Anything I can do?"

"Probably not. You fancy meeting up for a coffee tomorrow and being my listening ear?"

Oh my God! I felt my heart rate pick up a little and I shut my eyes. I kept them shut for a whole five seconds then opened them again and looked at the screen. Nope I wasn't imagining things. My hands shook even more as I replied.

"Sure I don't have plans, what did you have in mind?"

My reply looked all cool and calm but inside my head was screaming, 'YES, YES, YES!'

"How about Starbucks at twelve?"

"Sounds good to me. My pizza is ready so I'd better go."

"Ok Rox, see you tomorrow x."

"Byeee x."

I was beginning to think it was shaping up to be the best day ever, even my pizza and garlic bread with extra cheese tasted fantastic. I polished off everything on my plate then decided a long soak in the bath sounded just fabulous.

Chapter 12

I lounged lazily in my hot bath with a huge smile on my face. It was still sinking in that Brandon had actually asked me for coffee. Maybe he did like me, I thought. No, I told myself firmly. I couldn't think like that. He was way out of my league, in fact we were playing different sports altogether. I could be a really good friend to Brandon, that's it, that's all. I stepped out of the bath, dried myself with unnecessary vigour, wrapped a towel turban around my head and slipped into my jim jams and dressing gown I had left hanging over the radiator - mmmmm toastie warm pants!

I needed to occupy my brain so I decided to do some overdue research on Carrie's murder. I walked into my bedroom quite absentmindedly which was why I didn't see the old man standing in the middle of my floor till I was only a foot away from him.

I let out a startled gasp and nearly jumped out of my skin.

"I didna mean to startle ya hen," he said softly.

I realised I had seen the man before.

"I said hello to you in the bus stop today," I recalled. "You're a ghost?"

He looked to be around the same age as my Granda, he was as thin as a rake and he had the hugest ears I had ever seen. He looked like he was dressed for a night out, wearing a three-piece suit and a dicky bow. I felt even more sorry for Granda stuck in his slippers.

"Aye. I hope you don't mind that I followed you back here. You're the only one to talk to me."

"It's OK, I can try and help you if you like."

"Ya will? Just like that?"

"Sure. It's kind of my new vocation. Do you know what you need to do to pass over?"

"Yes."

"OK." I prepared myself for the worse. What would it be this time? Maybe I would have to break into the art museum or perhaps solve an ancient riddle. I was learning when it came to ghosts you never could tell.

"Well, me and my Eva never had much to speak of. That didn't matter though, we had each other. Over the years I've been hiding money, squirreling it away, but I died before I could tell her. Eva doesn't know anything about it and I just need to tell her that's all."

"OK, is that it?"

"Aye."

"That's easier than the last one that's for sure. What's your name?"

"Albert."

"I'm Roxanne but everyone calls me Roxy. How long have you been a ghost Albert?"

"Four weeks and two days."

"Ah, not long."

"No."

"Right well it's a bit late to go round now. Why don't you come back around eleven tomorrow and we'll go together OK?"

"You're a good girl quine."

"Thank you sir."

"I'll see you tomorrow."

He gave me an old wizened smile and disappeared with a pop. Well that introduction was better than the last, at least he hadn't startled me on the toilet like Carrie had. I sat in bed and read the local history books I had picked up from the library. I read and read until my eyes grew heavy and I had to admit defeat. I was still no nearer to solving the problem. The more I read the more I was convinced that I was missing something.

I tossed and turned all night and had the worse sleep I'd ever had. My mind was too occupied with other things. I gave up at 7am and got up. I didn't even get up that early on a school day never mind a Sunday!

I plodded grumpily to the kitchen and ate a huge bowl of chocolate cereal. I grabbed some juice and headed back through to carry on studying. This time I laid all the printouts and pictures I had gathered about Mr Ratchet on my bedroom carpet. The headlines from the paper jumped out at me.

'Girl of twelve goes missing' and 'Teachers questioned over disappearance of another'.

The details of some of the reports were absolutely sickening. When they found the little girls' bodies they discovered he'd burnt them with hot irons and other nasty deeds that I tried not to think about.

Shortly after ten Granda and Carrie appeared and they both had a read of all the articles on the floor. We were all totally stumped and my brain was frazzled.

I gave up and told them about my visit from Albert. The task to make him pass over seemed simple enough but I wanted my two ghostly companions to accompany me.

"You guys will come with me, yes?"

"Sure we will," Granda replied.

"I mean I'm going to look like a bit of an idiot anyway aren't I, turning up at someone's house and saying excuse me your late husband hid a wad of cash."

"It'll be fine."

"She's gonna think I'm nuts."

"Excuse me is it OK to come in?" The voice came from outside my bedroom door and I recognised Albert's wizened tones.

I opened the door, greeted him with a wide smile and invited him in. His face lit up when he saw Granda.

"Well I never. Finlay McDonald!"

"Albert my old boy when did you pop off."

"Granda!" I said totally shocked.

"Oh pooy," Granda replied.

"Just over four weeks, you?"

"Just over two weeks."

"What was it?"

"Heart. You?"

"Same."

I cleared my throat noisily.

"Oh sorry honey this is my old friend Albert. We worked together at Chevron you know. You actually met that time I took you in, don't you remember?"

"I was only five when you worked there."

"Really. It seems like yesterday to me."

"Would you like to go now?" I asked Albert.

"If you don't mind lass."

"Of course not. Do you live near by?"

"Aye, about fifteen minute walk."

Granda and Albert walked ahead chatting loudly and spouting the most colourful language. I was pretty sure that had Granda been alive, nana would have clipped his ear. I walked behind with Carrie leaving the two old men to their reminiscing.

"I love your Granda, Roxy. He's wonderful. I almost do not want to pass anymore," she said softly.

"I know. I love him to bits. He is just the perfect Granda in everyway. He draws a mean Popeye the Sailor man too. What do you two do all night?"

"Not much. We chat and we look around the school for
clues. Ghosts are mainly happy just to be most of the time.
An hour can feel like a minute sometimes."

"Have you really been on your own all this time?"

"Yes, I'm sure I've come across ghosts but it's not
always easy to spot one even for us."

"I really hope I can help you."

"You just try your best and that's good enough Rox."

We came to a complex of bungalows specially built for
the elderly. Each entrance had a little handrail outside and
some had wee window boxes.

"We are number seventeen," Albert said.

I took some deep breaths.

"Right, so where did you hide the money?"

"A loose floorboard on my side of the bed. It's all
bundled tightly in an old tea caddy."

"Cool. OK, I can do this."

I approached the front door and pressed the doorbell. At
first I thought no one was home or maybe the doorbell was
broken. I raised my hand to knock instead when I heard
shuffling from inside. The door opened a fraction and two
watery blue eyes stared back at me. When she saw it was
just a schoolgirl she opened it fully. Albert's wife looked to
be in her late seventies. She was wearing a black suit and
looked quite smartly dressed for a Sunday.

"Can I help you my dear?" she said softly.

"Yes, erm, are you Eva?"

"Yes dear."

"Well. I have a message for you. Now you might not believe me but please just check after I go anyway, OK?"

"I'm not following."

"Your husband hid some money in a tea caddy. It's under the loose floorboard on his side of the bed."

"How do you know?" Eva was now looking a little confused and slightly annoyed.

"I won't disturb you further, all I ask is that you check."

"I think I'll go inside now." And with that the front door was shut firmly in my face.

"She never believed in ghosts and she absolutely detests mediums," Albert said absent-mindedly.

"Well thanks a bloomin' much Albert. Forewarning would have been nice."

Deed done we made our way back to my flat.

"I need to change quickly then I have to go out," I told them.

"Yes I need to get back to the school," Carrie added.

"Albert my old chum, come and join us until the Mrs decides to look for your stash."

"Why not, it's a pity we can't have a wee dram."

"I know and I have bottles of the stuff in the garage."

The three ghosts walked me down to the main entrance of our flat and then they left. I bounded up the stairs to prepare for meeting Brandon. I meticulously straightened my hair and decided on a nice casual look; jeans, long deep red jumper and matching patent red slip-on shoes. I added a little teardrop pendant and a dash of cherry-flavoured lip gloss. I was so bloody nervous but I was as ready as I was ever going to be.

I set off enjoying the fresh air which calmed me down slightly. As I rounded the corner and Starbucks came into view I almost turned back. What if it was a big prank? What if he didn't show? All sorts of questions were running through my head but you don't get anything in life being afraid to take a chance. I opened the door and with a huge sigh of relief I saw Brandon sat in a large sofa. He had ordered two hot chocolates, two paninis and two huge slices of cake.

"What were you going to do if I didn't show?" I said pointing at the food.

"Probably eat it all myself." He grinned but I got the distinct impression that he was serious. I sat down next to him and picked a hot chocolate.

"Ooooooo, can I have the ham and cheese?"

"Sure." He offered me another heart-stopping grin.

"So what's on your mind?"

"I dumped Tiffany."

"Oh, because of me?"

"No, well, not just that, lots of stuff."

"I'm not being mean or anything but why did you go there in the first place?"

He took a bite of his chicken panini and a long slurp of hot chocolate.

"Like I said, we have a long history. It's turned into habit I guess. This is going to sound really bad but I sort of get a lot of female attention."

"Hmm, that had not escaped my notice."

"Well it does get pretty bad. I had to take a restraining order out on one girl."

"Really! Cool, who was it?"

"I don't want to say OK, but the point is it's not as bad when I'm unavailable and Tiff is pretty protective."

"Hmm, you mean possessive?"

"Lately yes but she sort of keeps everyone else at bay. That does sound bad doesn't it?" he winced.

"So what you are trying to tell me is that you keep old Tiff on your arm to keep the others from sniffing around."

"Yes, I am a bad person."

"I'm not gonna lie," I said eating a bit of my Panini. "It sounds bad but it makes sense in a vain sort of way."

"Quiet," he laughed.

"Still, Tiffany is one on her own."

"You are not wrong there. You know she used to be such a nice girl, I don't know what happened the last year or so. She's started smoking and last month she went to a party and got so drunk the police took her home. She's developed a real vicious streak too and I have a feeling I'll be finding chilli peppers in my Speedos."

I nearly sprayed the table next to us with hot chocolate.

"Speedos?"

"You've got to be streamlined."

I burst out laughing but the image of Brandon in a pair of tight Speedos was firmly branded into my brain.

Like our last visit to Starbucks the conversation was easy. He was so nice to be around and he really seemed to be enjoying my company. I wished at that moment Annabel or Jennifer could have looked in because I was sure that I was being flirted with, especially when we started on the cakes. Mine was a carrot cake and Brandon's was a huge passion fruit one.

"Oh my God you have to try this Rox." He cut off a slice with his fork and held it up to my mouth. I looked at it slightly taken aback.

"It's OK, I'm germ free," he smiled and I accepted the cake.

"Mmmmmm, wow that is nice."

"You are so easy to talk to Roxanne."

"You too."

"You going to this Halloween dance?"

"Probably not. I never go to things like that."

"Really, why?"

"Lack of date."

"So you've never had a boyfriend around the time of a dance."

"Nope." I smiled nervously. "I've never had a boyfriend."

"Wow, really? That surprises me Rox."

"Us geeks don't have 'em queuing up like you jock types."

"Well. How about I take you?"

"What?"

"Well I mean if you want?"

I was pretty sure that everyone in a six foot vicinity of our table could hear my heart pounding wildly in my chest.

"You mean like a date?" I asked.

"Sure, it'll be fun."

"Its ages away," I laughed trying to cover my nervousness. "You may have another floozy repeller by then."

"Definitely not, but I would withhold from telling everyone for a few days. Tiffany is pretty annoyed at the moment."

"Ooooo, so I'm your little secret too huh?"

"Now you're making it sound wrong"

I elbowed him playfully.

"Ow, you are as solid as a rock Brandon."

"And you are so little Rox, like one of those munchkins."

"Hey!"

"Kidding, kidding." He threw his hands up defensively. "Munchkins are cute though," he grinned.

"Well, OK I'd love to go. Don't worry I'll keep it to myself."

After a second cup of hot chocolate along with plenty of giggles and jokes, I was surprised to find that it was three 'o' clock. I was literally walking on air as Brandon walked me home. I was being taken to the ball by a fabulously gorgeous boy but I couldn't help being confused by the situation. I mean we weren't going out and I got the distinct impression that he was taking me to the ball as a favour to a friend sort of thing. But there had been definite flirting with the feeding of the cake and sexy grins over the marshmallow-topped hot chocolate.

We said our goodbyes as we reached the flat and before I knew what was happening he leaned forward and gave me a hug. He smelt so good like he'd spent a lot of time outdoors. The hug lingered on for a lot longer than a normal goodbye friendly hug, I didn't want to be the one to break away but we couldn't hug in the street all day. He took a deep breath and exhaled slowly.

"Thanks for today Rox, you've really cheered me up. See you tomorrow."

I watched him walk away. My heart told me to run to him, tell him how I felt and my head told me not to be so stupid. I usually listened to my head.

Once in the solitude of my bedroom I gazed at myself in the mirror. Was there something different about me? Along with my ability to talk to the dead had I picked a new pheromone brand?

Brandon had always been friendly and polite but something had changed, something had shifted. I had waited all this time for him, never having the courage to make a move. Always being the friend to ask about homework and now could I possibly become his…I didn't want to say it… girlfriend.

For once I let my mind wander fully and I imagined us walking down Union Street hand in hand or perhaps bowling down at the beach. Normal things that people did on dates without giving it too much thought. I'd never been asked out on one.

Then I started to panic a little. What the hell was I going to wear to the ball? I didn't even own a dress pretty enough to wear to a ball. Shoes weren't a problem, mum had brought me a lovely pair of kitten heel shoes in Warehouse during the summer holidays, they'd been on sale at half price.

I would have to dip into my savings and maybe visit the posh dress bit in Debenhams. I decided against rushing out to buy a fancy dress. The ball was four weeks away and I couldn't shake the feeling that he would probably have found someone else by then, someone prettier and more experienced. I hoped he was a good guy through and through and wouldn't break my heart.

Chapter 13

When Monday morning came I was awake, showered and dressed before my alarm clock went off. Mum looked at me in amazement from the living room as I practically danced to the kitchen and made my breakfast.

"You're full of beans this morning Rox."

"Yip, I was just wide awake, no point in lying in bed. You want tea mum?"

"Sure. You have got to see this on the news. Some widow in Aberdeen found some money her husband had hidden in the house while he was alive."

"Really? Cool." I smiled. Eva had found the money so Albert must surely have passed over.

"Yes get this though, they'd never had much money but he'd managed to hide away fifty grand. His wife thinks it was winnings from the horses."

I nearly choked on my cinnamon bagel.

"Fifty grand!"

"Yes can you believe it? Fifty pound notes all rolled up in an old tea caddy."

"Thanks for sharing the wealth Albert," I muttered under my breath.

"Some people have all the luck. Can you imagine if your Granda had done that?"

I took a seat next to mum and watched the news as it came on. Eva was being interviewed and she had obviously dressed to impress for her five minutes of fame, wearing a matching coral pink skirt and jacket suit.

"How did you come to find this stash of money Mrs Simmons?"

"Well the floorboard squeaked you see and it was loose. I was going to nail it down and I lifted it first and saw the old tea caddy."

Well there you go, I was an unsung hero. Eva obviously didn't want to admit what had really happened. The front door buzzer sounded and I got up, gave mum a kiss on the cheek and headed down stairs.

I was absolutely dying to tell my two best friends about my afternoon date with Brandon. It was on the tip of my tongue to shout out that he had asked me to the ball but I held back. Why? I trusted my friends but I guess if Brandon changed his mind then I wouldn't look foolish if no one knew. It was hard to mask my happiness. Annabel and Jennifer commented on it several times on the short walk to school.

"I'm just in a good mood guys!"

"How can you be in a good mood with double maths today?" Annabel asked.

"Easy, I lurve maths," I replied.

"You are weird you know that Rox, W-E-I-R-D, weird."

"Oh come on Jennifer loves maths just as much as I do."

"Hey don't bring me into your maths fetish."

"No you have a Mr Winters fetish," I teased.

"Hey! I wouldn't call it a fetish, more a…"

"Obsession?"

"Exactly. No wait!"

We burst out laughing, my mood was infectious. Granda and Carrie were dutifully waiting outside the school gates and they followed us inside. After registration I headed for the toilet while Annabel and Jennifer went on to class. Granda and Carrie followed me.

"Oh my God," I exclaimed when I had checked the bathroom was empty. "I can't believe Albert had fifty grand under his floorboards."

"Fifty, five zero fifty?" Granda replied equally shocked.

"It was on the news. When did he pass?"

"It was about two," Carrie said.

"Well that's that. At least I didn't have to steal anything this time."

I was pretty sure that nothing was going to bring me down and I was on a high all day. Even the sight of Tiffany standing outside our maths class with all the other students waiting for Mr Winters couldn't dampen my mood.

"Look here comes the scab," she sneered as I passed her.

I rolled my eyes and walked past her to join the back of the queue. Tiffany stuck her arm out and stopped me. I looked at her and saw the sheer look of hatred on her face.

"You think you've split us up. You haven't you know. This is just a minor tiff."

"Tiffany, move your hand out of my way and for the record, I don't actually give a crap."

"I'd watch your back."

"With people like you around I always do."

I pushed past her arm and Jennifer and I joined the back of the queue. I was pretty sure the essence wouldn't have to work too hard if he wanted to possess Tiffany she was already a grade 'A' cowbag.

When Mr Winters appeared Jennifer let out an audible sigh and we all took our seats. Brandon came in last and gave me a little smile.

All through the lesson when I was trying to concentrate on Pythagoras, Brandon kept catching my eye and giving me sly little winks. I fought the urge to blush several times and twice Jennifer asked me if I was OK. Mr Winters seemed in high spirits and commented on the improvement in Brandon's work and I couldn't help but feel a little proud. Maybe I could hatch a plan and pretend I couldn't swim. See if he would teach me. Good plan in theory but I was pretty sure seeing Brandon in a pair of Speedos would tip me over the edge mentally.

At the end of the lesson three of Brandon's rugby friends popped their heads round the door and whisked him away. I didn't see him for the rest of the day. My mood deflated slightly, but only slightly. I was just glad the next day was Tuesday which meant after school I would have him all to myself, that put the smile on my face. I walked home with Annabel and Jennifer half in a dream and I was glad to have the house all to myself when I got home. Mum had taken a week off for Granda's funeral and then an extra week to see nana settled. Mum is a physiotherapist up at the hospital.

I clicked on the computer and grabbed a bag of Quavers while it booted up. I sat down and munched while I checked my emails and messages on Facebook. No messages and Brandon had rugby practice, I remembered from when I saw his timetable so I knew he wouldn't be in for a while.

I chatted idly to Jennifer who had also logged on and was bugging everyone for Farmville nails to build a stable. I obliged and fertilized her crops too, I was a good friend.

I minimized Facebook and then browsed idly through various websites I thought might help me find Carrie's body. Nothing, nada. It was all the same articles or opinions that weren't based on any fact whatsoever. The task seemed more impossible every day. I was yet to find out what the layout of the school was nearly seventy years ago; that sort of thing was not readily available.

At least for now Carrie seemed happy with Granda for company. A little popping sound interrupted my thoughts. I maximized my Facebook screen thinking it was Jennifer either thanking me for the nails or wanting to prattle on some more about Mr Winter's lovely long hair. I was shocked and pleased to see it was actually Brandon.

"Hi."

A big smile spread across my face as I replied.

"Hey you."

"I wanted to speak to you today but just didn't have the chance."

"Oh, wat about?"

"I dunno, I wonder if I left you confused on Sunday. If it was weird you know, us going to the dance together."

I thought carefully about my wording before typing.

"I got the impression you were taking me because I haven't been before."

It seemed like ages till he replied.

"Well I sort of wanted to ask you anyway."

OK now I was palpitating and my palms had gone sweaty. Was he saying what I thought he was saying?

"What do you mean?"

"I mean… damn, I hate typing stuff like this. It's only early, do you wanna go eat?"

"Sure."

"I'll swing by yours in 45 mins, OK?"

"Brill."

"See you soon."

I shut the computer down, fell off the swivel chair, jumped up, smoothed down my hair and felt glad that I was on my own. Forty-five minutes was cutting it fine. I jumped in the shower where I scrubbed myself at super speed, then blasted my hair dry and straightened it like there was no tomorrow.

Granda and Carrie chose that moment to pop into the room. I was sat at my vanity table applying some lip gloss and choosing which earrings to wear.

"You going out love?" Granda asked.

"Yes. Brandon wants to meet up for something to eat. I think it's a maths thing."

"Roxanne, you always were a rubbish liar. Does this boy like you?"

"I don't know Granda. He's asked me to the Halloween dance."

Granda frowned.

"This is where it starts you know."

"Granda."

"This is why girls are getting pregnant."

I scoffed.

"Oh come on Granda. I've never had a boyfriend OK, ever. Studies come first and all that. It's a dance and I've never been asked to one before. Don't you trust me?"

He softened a little.

"You're right honey, you have always been a sensible girl."

"Thanks."

"He's special you know, that Brandon boy," Carrie added.

"Pipe down in the back," I said and Carrie sniggered.

"Look we'll probably grab a pizza then I'm gonna do some research and if you guys want you can do some more reading."

Both faces lit up.

"Right I've got to go. I'll wait downstairs for him."

I quickly scribbled a note for mum and scooted out the door before any more questions could be thrown my way.

Chapter 14

I saw Brandon approaching from the top of the street and set off to meet him halfway. My stomach did somersaults just watching the way he walked. What was wrong with me? He just walked with such confidence and grace; it made me feel so awkward and nerdy. He waved as we got closer and I quickened my pace slightly eager to be within speaking distance. He looked so handsome in faded jeans, a tight Quiksilver t-shirt and he wore tennis-type trainers that were crispy white. He looked way older than fifteen.

"Hi, you look nice Rox," he said it with a genuine smile and I looked down at myself to double-check. I had chosen a pair of black leggings and one of my nicer jumpers, it was long, thick and cream with a high neck and wide tan belt. I had teamed it with a pair of flat black slip on shoes with a buckle on the front. Overall I'd have said I wasn't looking too bad either.

"Thanks, you look great too."

God I was nervous. Why did he have to smile like that?

"Where do you want to eat?"

"No idea, how about Pizza Hut?"

"I was thinking a bit more up market than that. How about the pizza restaurant at the top of Union Street?"

"Sure if you like but they are pricey there."

"Hey I'm paying, no buts."

We walked side by side. Brandon told me he had a really big rugby game coming up and their coach was pressurising them to commit all their spare time to practice, that was why his rugby mates had dragged him off right after maths.

"But don't worry, we are still on for tomorrow. You wanna go straight to Starbucks, study there."

"Well, I could do with stopping by the library for a little while but then we could go."

We reached the restaurant and Brandon opened the door for me like a proper gentlemen. The waitress seated us in a secluded corner and handed us a menu each to browse. I opted for a small Hawaiian pizza, and Brandon ordered the biggest one with everything on it.

"Oh my God, are you actually going to eat all that yourself?" I chuckled.

"Yup and we are having dessert too."

"No way!"

"Yes way."

A few minutes of silence followed as I summoned up the courage to probe Brandon further about our Facebook chat. Thank God he took the first step.

"Sorry about earlier online. You know it's so easy to type talk to someone but, oh I don't know, I just prefer to get it out in the open."

"OK, this sounds serious should I be worried?"

"No, not at all. Well, it's just, I like you Rox. I wanted you to know I'm not taking you to the dance because you've never been. I asked you because I like you."

"I'm sorry, come again?"

"I like you," he laughed, looked at me and then laughed harder. "Rox there's no need to look so shocked."

"You, like me?"

"Why do you look so surprised?"

"No one ever likes me," I lowered my voice to a whisper. "I'm a geek"

"Roxy even if you were a geek, which you're not, I like you for you. You're funny, kind and pretty too."

I wished the waitress hadn't taken my menu away. I was desperate for something to hide behind so he couldn't see my cheeks flaming red.

"I don't know what to say. I mean I like you too."

"Thank God. I've been as nervous as hell building up the courage to ask you out."

"You are joking right? You can get any girl you want."

"But I want you."

I tried to remain calm, I had questions but I didn't want to scare him away.

"How do I know you aren't using me to enhance your math's ability, eh?"

"Well I have a slight confession."

"Oooooooo really." I relaxed a little and sat back in my chair.

"Well, how many pi decimals can you recite?"
"Hmm, well at a push five or six lemmie think."

"3.14159265358979323846264633383"

"OK, OK, I get the picture. So what, you were pretending to be bad at maths?"

"Yes, are you mad?"

"No just confused why didn't you just ask me out?"

"I was scared you'd just think I was a lame vain fret boy and laugh in my face."

"Awwwwwww. You aren't lame but you are pretty vain," I said jokingly.

"Hey! I don't think that because you're a teenage girl you should smell like BO and Clearasil."

"Alright, I'm sorry." I held my hands up in surrender.

He looked at me and his expression turned serious.

"So you wanna give it a go, me and you?"

"And you're sure it's not a joke, or a bet you have on with someone?"

"God no! Rox don't put yourself down. You are a wonderful person."

If it was possible I blushed even deeper.

"I think I'd like to give it a go. It will take a while to sink in. One thing though."

"What's that?"

"I want it kept a secret for now OK? Tiffany already has it in for me."

"I'm happy to shout it from the rafters," he grinned.

"Not just yet, let's eat first."

"OK."

The pizza was fabulous. It could have tasted like rubbish but it would have still been fabulous. I kept pinching myself under the table because I was convinced I was led at home in my bed dreaming and any minute I was going to wake up. I began to think, that if this was real, if the impossible had happened and Brandon and I were an item well, there'd be kissing…hopefully. I'd never kissed a boy before. If there was a God, I thought, he'd better make me a good kisser because I'd been a really good girl. I studied hard and was kind to old people too, so he should at least cut me some slack in the lip-locking department.

I watched in total disbelief as Brandon scoffed his way through his entire pizza which was loaded with so much topping you could hardly see cheese. He talked with his mouth full too. It didn't put me off one bit. It made him more normal, more human. He saw me looking at his empty plate in disbelief.

"I have a big appetite."

"How can you eat so much and stay so… so toned."

"Rubgy practice twice a week and swimming once a week. I run most mornings if I can. Newburgh Beach is serene at first light."

"Wow."

"What?"

"You; running on a beach at dawn. I can just imagine it. Your hair flapping in the wind and everything, just like a shampoo advert. Next you'll be telling me you volunteer at the PDSA, cuddling sick kittens at the weekend."

"Are you mocking me?"

"Just a little."

"I think I can handle you but I have the last laugh."

"Oh yeah?"

"You laugh at my appetite and hair well if we go the distance you'll be the one feeding me."

"Er, this is only our first date and you can feed yourself!"

The walk home was even more surreal. As we rounded the corner onto my street Brandon slipped his hand into mine. It was warm and dry and the action felt totally natural and right. I couldn't believe the boy I had liked for so many years was holding my hand and walking me home. We were an item, we were together. It had been so easy, as easy as 'you want to give it a go'. I just wanted to keep it quiet until Tiffany simmered down and I had the chance to actually believe it myself. With all the ghost-solving problems going on, I didn't really want Tiffany vowing revenge on me too.

All too soon we were stood outside my flat and it was time to say goodbye. I was petrified he was going to try to kiss me.

"Well thanks for pizza," I said.

"You are most welcome. I'll see you tomorrow and then we'll have our extra tuition as planned."

He gave my hand a gentle squeeze, bent and brushed my cheek lightly with his lips which made me shiver. Brandon then flashed me a wicked smile before he turned and started up the street. I watched him for a few seconds, touching my cheek where his lips had caressed me, then with a sigh I entered our building.

There could have been twenty thousand steps up to my front door it wouldn't have mattered because I floated all the way there. Mum was in the kitchen sipping a mug of tea by the window. I bounded over gave her a big kiss and started to do the washing up.

"Who is he?" Mum asked with a suspicious tone.

"What?"

"You're a happy kid Roxy but not that happy, so it must be a boy. Am I right?"

"Sort of," I grinned "But you can't say anything to Annabel and Jennifer OK."

"Why?"

"Coz, he just broke up with his girlfriend so we are taking it slow and I don't want her to find out because she's meaner than hell."

"You can hold your own, if I taught you nothing else it's to stick up for yourself"

"Oh I'm not scared of her but I don't see the point in aggravating the situation."

"Well you've always been a sensible girl Roxy so be careful now. Well let's have some hot chocolate and you can tell me all about him."

Help my Granda is Haunting Me!

I spent a little time with mum that evening and headed through to bed about ten. I picked the evening paper up and took it with me. Granda and Carrie were waiting with eager anticipation of the read I had promised them. I set the paper out for Granda and opened *Harry Potter* once more for Carrie. I had far more horrible things to contend with. I once again opened my Mr Ratchet folder and began idly looking over the articles.

"I'm loving this book," Carrie said happily.

I was happy to work while Granda and Carrie read but after half an hour I was tired and cranky.

"You guys," I said. "I'm struggling with this. I'm going over the same stuff again and again. I'm at a total dead end."

"You want me to help honey?" Granda asked.

"Please, will you just look over everything I've highlighted and tell me if there's anything I've missed?"

I showed him everything, the newspaper articles, the pictures and the bits from the library books too. I gave him time to read each article and by the time we were through he was as equally baffled as me and it was nearly midnight.

"There's something there," he said.

"I know, I can't put my finger on it."

"Well we just need to persevere. It's really getting late. Carrie, are you ready to go honey?"

She looked up from her book and nodded.

"Granda it's so nice of you to spend every night at that place," I said.

"It's not so bad. We sometimes go over and see your nana for a couple of hours or we go down to the beach and watch the waves."

"Awwww."

"I'm never lonely or sad now," Carrie said happily.

I wasn't the least bit jealous of how close the two of them had become, in fact I was beginning to look upon Carrie as a little sister. She looked so innocent and it was horrible to think that she had been rattling around the school for all those years. She deserved a Granda and she deserved one as good as mine.

When the two flashed out of the room leaving me alone with my thoughts I decided to get some much-needed sleep. I brushed my teeth, slipped into my jammies and crawled into bed. I thought about the days ahead where I would have to act normal. It was hard enough acting normal when there were ghosts following me around but now I had to act like I wasn't totally walking on air, fantastically happy. It was going to be tough. Secretly I would be wearing the biggest smile because I, Roxanne May McDonald, had a boyfriend. But not just any boyfriend; I had Brandon.

Chapter 15

"Morning Roxy."

I was cleansing my face with a babywipe when I heard Carrie's girlish voice fill the air around me. A second later she popped into the room.

"Hey, where's Granda?"

"Well he went to see your Nana last night and she was a little upset so he is spending the day out there he didn't want to leave her."

"Oh, I'd better see if I can get mum to go see her."

I went through to the kitchen and found mum making me scrambled eggs.

"Morning sweetheart. You want cheese on these?"

"Please mum. Erm mum, are you working today?"

"Half day today sweetie I start at twelve, why?"

"Do you think you could go and see nana this morning before you go in?"

"Why, what's the matter?"

"I'm probably just being really silly but I just have a feeling. I mean I could always take a half a day off, say I have the dentist."

"Never think you're being silly Roxy honey. It's lovely that you worry about her. I'll go after my tea OK?"

"Thanks mum."

I scoffed down my breakfast just as Jennifer and Annabel announced their arrival with a buzz of the door.

"Bye honey and don't let this new boyfriend of yours affect your grade."

"I know mum, I won't. See you when you get home.

Annabel and Jennifer were waiting outside for me they must have seen the concerned look on my face because they both asked me if everything was alright at the same time as each other. I wasn't alright; I didn't like to think about Nana being on her own and all upset..

"Just a bit worried about Nana."

"How is she doing?"

"Really well considering but she's all on her own and I just worry about her."

We made our usual pit stop for hot chocolate and as we were ten minutes early we sat down.

"We should do something fun this weekend guys," Jennifer said.

"Ooooooo sounds good, what you thinking?" I replied.

"We should go bowling." Jennifer suggested.

"I'm brasic," Annabel sighed.

"Well how about a sleepover then?"

"Yeah, that's a fab idea," I said.

"Cool with me," Annabel nodded.

"Well we'll have it at mine and I'll get my dad to order Chinese."

Help my Granda is Haunting Me!

Carrie was waiting at the entrance to the school and followed behind us. There was still no sign of Granda. We made a detour to the bathroom where my two best friends had previously gone all possessed on my ass, which left me slightly shaken but nothing, thank God, happened. I passed Brandon on the way to registration and he gave me a subtle little wink and I smiled back. I don't know how he did it but he made our disgusting green uniform look fashionable and it was all I could do to stop myself swooning. I tried my best to keep from grinning like an idiot and instead look cool and nonchalant; I think I succeeded…ish.

The day couldn't pass fast enough and when it was time to head for art, I was just a little nervous. Annabel and I walked together while Jennifer went off to a different class. We waited patiently for the teacher and I watched everyone coming around the corner hoping to see Brandon before class started. I only had just over an hour to wait until we were by ourselves but I ached for him already. Then my worst nightmare came round the corner, nope not Mr Ratchet with a machete but Tiffany. Her eyes met mine and her face contorted into a look of such hatred that I was momentarily shocked.

I hate personal confrontation, I avoid it whenever I can and I keep my head down but when someone is out to get you there's nothing you can do and Tiffany was well and truly after my blood.

"This is all your fault you know," she curled her lip.

"What is?"

"Brandon of course, he won't even talk to me now. You stupid ugly bitch."

"Hey Tiffany there's no need for that." Annabel came to my defence.

"Shut up you saddo, you've got your head so far up ugly here's ass, that I bet you can taste her frizzy hairdo."

"Don't flaming push it," I growled feeling my blood start to boil.

"And what the hell are you gonna do huh, you think because you finally discovered straighteners that you can get a back bone too? Geeks are at the bottom of the social pile and you need to know your place."

I snapped, God forgive, me but I snapped. I felt this rage bubble up from the tip of my toes and flush through my whole body. I grabbed a fistful of the front of her shirt swung her around and slammed her into the wall. She visibly panicked at my anger induced strength.

"I am through taking this crap, three bloody years you've been throwing your weight around. NO MORE!" She was now nervously glancing to see if anyone in line would come to her defence, no one did.

"Brandon dumped you because you are a complete and utter cow. That's the reason not anything or anyone else, just you. Now stay the hell away from me."

Utterly defeated and humiliated she nodded and as I released the front of her shirt I saw I had actually been holding her about an inch off the ground She looked at me in complete disbelief then without another word silently joined the back of the queue.

Everyone waiting for class began to whisper furiously and Annabel had this big stupid grin on her face.

"What?"

"I have wanted to do that for years," she said. "How did it feel?"

"Fabulous, perhaps she'll get off my case now."

"I don't think you have anything to worry . I think I visibly saw her ego shrink."

"It's never nice resorting to violence though."

"She had it coming."

"Maybe, maybe."

Our art teacher rounded the corner, opened the door and we all found a desk. Brandon jogged in and apologised to the teacher saying the gym teacher had kept him back to talk about something. He smiled and took a seat to my right; well away from Tiffany who was smiling sweetly and trying to catch his eye. I smiled silently to myself, if only she knew.

Jennifer was waiting at the bottom of the stairs after class and we filled her in about the Tiffany incident. Annabel greatly exaggerated everything and looking back I couldn't believe I'd had the strength and courage to do such a thing.

"Well it's about time, don't you go feeling bad Rox, I know you too well." She said.

Brandon who had stayed behind in class came down the stairs and bounded over to me.

"Hey Rox."

"Hi."

"Hi Brandon," Jennifer and Annabel said.

"We were just leaving, weren't we Annabel?"

My subtle friends left the two of us alone.

"There will have to be a slight change of plan, if that's OK."

"Sure, what's up?"

"Coach Mckinnon's driving me bonkers. He wants the team in for an hour to practice for a big match we have on Saturday."

"That's fine we can meet another time."

"It'll only take like, an hour or two, tops. I could swing by your place after if your parents don't mind."

"There's just me and my mum and she won't mind. Do you want something to eat?"

"Is that OK? I was going to grab a chipper."

"Nah, I'll sort you something out."

"You're the best. I'll see you around five."

Mum was sat watching telly when I got in, usually when she worked a half day she was there till five so I was a little concerned.

"Hi honey, how was your day?" she greeted warmly.

"It was OK."

"I thought you had study after school with Brandon," she smiled.

"He has to go to the gym. I said it was OK for him to come here after. Is that OK?"

"Of course."

"How was nana?"

"A little upset actually, I haven't been into work. I called in sick and spent the day there."

"Poor nana."

"She'll have days like this, it's only a few days really since he died and they were together for so long."

"I know mum, how are you?"

"I'm OK, I'm doing fine, really. Come on, I know I only just filled the fridge but why don't we order Chinese, does Brandon like Chinese."

"He eats like a horse mum."

"That's OK but he's not stealing all the crunchy fried prawns."

"Deal. I'll go get my homework done now."

"Sure Rox."

I was about half way through when Granda appeared.

"Hi Rox."

"Hi Granda. How's nana?"

"She was affa bad last night. She kept crying and talking to me."

"You know Granda, perhaps we should tell her about you."

"You think?"

"Yes, I mean she loves that Colin Fry guy, she's been to see him twice. I think we should tell her."

"I just worry it will somehow come back to bite you."

146

"If I have you there I will be able to tell her stuff that only you could possibly know."

"Let me think OK?"

"What's to think about?"

"Well if we leave it she will grieve and then it will be easy for her. If we tell her she will know that I am there but she can never see me, speak to me or touch me."

"Ah, I didn't think of it like that."

"So you see she might initially get some comfort from the fact that I am here but in the long run it will probably do more harm than good."

"I think you might be right. Where's Carrie?"

"With her auntie; she lives in a care home at the other side of town."

"Oh is she coming by later?"

"Yes, when she needs to go back I told her to come here first."

"Cool well mum's ordering takeaway and I picked you up a paper on the way home so I can spread it out a bit on the bed if you want to read."

"That would be good Roxy."

I carried on working and when requested turned the pages for Granda. I heard mum phoning for takeaway at around four thirty and I was counting the minutes down till Brandon arrived. I wasn't disappointed. At ten minutes past five the door buzzed. I heard mum pad through and ask who it was over the intercom and then she knocked lightly on my door saying.

"Roxy, your friend is here."

Granda grinned like a Cheshire cat.

"Awwwww quine, you're blushing."

"Quiet Granda. If I'm not back through by the time you have to go I'll see you tomorrow." I kissed the air at the side of his cheek.

"OK honey," he chuckled.

I only had to wait a few seconds before there was a light rapping on the front door and I opened it to Brandon.

"Hi, sorry it took a bit longer than I thought."

"That's OK mum has ordered takeaway."

"Ooooooooooo, Chinese?"

"Yes, come on through." He followed me to the living room at the end of the hallway. It was a fairly big room. The kitchen was just off it and this was where the table was, but mum had popped two plates and forks on the coffee table along with glasses of lemonade for us. On cue she came in from the kitchen.

"Mum this is Brandon."

"Hello there, it's nice to meet you."

"You too, Mrs McDonald." The front door buzzed once more.

"Call me Pam, that'll be the Chinese, I hope you're hungry guys."

"Always," Brandon grinned.

We sat side by side on the sofa while mum let the delivery man up with our food and paid him. She took it straight into the kitchen and returned quickly placing the takeaway bag on the table next to the plates.

"I've got mine so I'll leave you both to it. I'll go watch TV in my bedroom."

"You don't have to do that mum."

"It's fine, not too late on a school night though, OK?"

"Yes mum."

I dug into the bag and placed all the dishes onto the coffee table. I flipped the top off each one and we started loading our plates. Mum, as promised wandered past with her takeaway on a tray and went through to her bedroom, shutting the door softly after her.

"This is great, I love Chinese food."

"Why does that not surprise me?"

"I couldn't wait to talk to you, one of the guys at practice said you had a run-in with Tiff. Are you OK?"

"I'm OK, she just pushed it too far is all," I grabbed a spare rib and nibbled it as daintily as I could.

"Maybe you were right about not letting her know. I don't want you getting extra hassle on my account."

"I can handle her but there's no point in aggravating her is there. So how was practice?"

"Brutal, we'll be lucky if there's a team left at this rate, but never mind."

"You have a pretty packed schedule."

"I know but it's nothing I can't handle, you mind if I finish that?" He indicated with his fork to the rest of the food sitting in the containers. I laughed.

"Be my guest. So do I need a big fancy dress for the ball?"

"Of course I'll be wearing my kilt."

"Get out!"

"Seriously, it's a big thing. Well it's big if you want it to be and I plan on pulling out all the stops so yes you'll need a big fancy dress."

"I'm all nervous."

"Don't be, you'll look gorgeous whatever you wear."

I blushed.

"It was hard today in art. I wanted to sit next to you and tell you how happy I was and stuff."

"I know me too. I've got to say I'm still in disbelief about it all but why don't we just play it down till the dance, it's only four weeks away."

"Four weeks!"

"Yes, that'll give Tiffany chance to move on and you will probably be well bored of me by then."

"Why do you say that?"

"Honestly?" I asked. He nodded. "It's just that you've had a lot of girlfriends and I haven't had any boyfriends. I'm worried that things won't move as fast as you'd like them to and you'll get bored waiting. It doesn't matter how much I like you, I have to do this at a pace I feel comfortable with."

"Listen Roxy, just because I've had a lot of girlfriends doesn't necessarily mean that I've done heaps of stuff. I haven't done as much as you might think and I don't want you to think that I'd ever pressurise you, OK? We'll move as slow as you like. I feel comfortable with you; I feel I could tell you anything."

"Like what?" I laughed.

"Have you ever had a secret you couldn't tell anyone?"

"Maybe," I frowned, this was sounding serious.

"I do. It's nothing bad so don't fret, but I feel I could tell you now and you would hold it in your heart and never betray me. I've never felt like that before towards another hum…person."

"You can trust me Brandon."

"I know, but I'm just not quite ready to tell all, not just yet."

"I understand."

"You're expression says differently"

"I was just thinking about what it could possibly be."

"My secret?"

"Yes."

"Just gimmie a little time and I'll open up. I've liked you for a long time Rox but you just seemed so unattainable."

"Me unattainable, you are kidding right?"

"Why do you do that?"

"What?"

"Put yourself down."

"I'm not, I'm just a realist."

"I'll prove you wrong when we arrive at the dance together. You got anything for dessert?"

"Oh my God you can't possibly eat anything else?"

"I can, that was a tiny portion."

"I think we have cheesecake in the fridge."

"Bring it on."

I was stuffed. I took our empty plates through to the kitchen and sliced Brandon a generous serving of American cheese cake. We flicked through the channels on the satellite TV and decided on *Transformers 2*, one of my all-time favourite movies. It turned out to be one of Brandon's too. As the credits rolled, mum popped her head round the door and politely said we should call it a night. I was surprised to find it was half past nine.

"Thanks for tea Pam," he said getting his mobile out of his pocket.

"I'll take you home Brandon," Mum offered.

"You sure?"

"No prob, let me grab my keys. You coming Roxy?"

"Sure."

We all piled downstairs and into mum's little Saxo. Brandon and I sat in the back and he gave mum directions to a new set of luxury apartments at the top of Queen Street in the posh end of town. I remembered them being built because the starting price was a quarter of a million pounds.

"Wow, what do your parents do Brandon?" asked mum.

"My dad is an architect and my stepmum is a home designer."

"Those apartments are beautiful."

All too soon we were pulling into the car park. Brandon gave my hand a squeeze.

"I'll see you in morning Rox, thanks for dinner Pam."
"Anytime honey."

"See you tomorrow," I replied.

He stood at the door to his apartment and as we drove away I saw him remove his keys and let himself in.

"He seems like a very nice young man Roxy."

"He is mum."

"You just be careful."

"I will, don't worry mum."

"I know you will honey. Let's get home eh, you certainly know how to pick 'em Rox, he is certainly easy on the eyes."

"Mum!"

Chapter 16

Over the next few days my life took a tremendous turn and I became two different people. There was sensible Roxanne who went to school and did her work and this new Roxanne who was in love and besotted.

I was constantly on the verge of screaming out that Brandon and I were a couple even though I still had doubts myself. Tiffany made it more than clear she absolutely and categorically hated me in every way. She didn't say it in words but whenever I was in the vicinity she wore an expression like someone had smeared something nasty under her nose.

Brandon's schedule was annoyingly packed. He had swimming once a week after school and he had extra rugby too. I didn't want his academic life to be affected by our budding relationship so I refused to let him bunk off any extracurricular activities. He spent every night at our house and mum soon adored him. He fitted into my life as if he had been destined to be there.

Towards the end of the school week, Brandon and I were sat together on two floor cushions eating a family sized bag of Revels and watching TV. Granda was through in my bedroom reading a newspaper I'd spread out on my bed,

Carrie had gone to see relatives and Mum was making spaghetti bolognaise. We were watching an episode of *Buffy the Vampire Slayer*, another one of my secret likes.

"This has got to be the lamest program ever, why do you like it?" Brandon asked as Buffy back flipped across the screen, sword in hand and decapitated an angry vampire.

"She's super cool and Angel is so nice."

"She looks like she needs feeding."

"I swear to God Brandon you need counselling, you are obsessed with food."

"I like my food."

"Really, I hadn't noticed!"

He gave me a playful shove with his shoulder.

"Tea will be ten minutes guys," mum shouted from the kitchen.

"You got garlic bread Pam?"

"Yup, one baguette or two?"

"Two." Brandon looked over and smiled at me as I rolled my eyes.

Ten minutes later the three of us were sat at the kitchen table and mum was positively beaming at the sheer amount of food Brandon was ploughing through (he managed a whole garlic bread to himself).

"I love to see a young man eating," she said fondly.

"That was great," Brandon replied using a slice of the second garlic bread to mop up the sauce from his plate.

"I'm glad you thought so. I'm going to nip out to Nana's." She loaded our dishes into the dishwasher. "Not too late honey."

"OK mum."

"No problems Pam."

"There are custard slices in the fridge."

Brandon shot out of the chair and was in the fridge. He was totally at home, it was wonderful.

We grabbed a custard slice each even though I felt like I were going to burst and we settled down in front of the TV. I flicked idly through the channels and stopped briefly on the local news. The news presenter was stood in front of the Beach Ballroom, a notorious spot for young joy riders.

"Shortly after eight yesterday evening a young lady, Michelle Kingsley, was knocked down by an unknown vehicle. A passer-by found Michelle and she was rushed to Forester Hill Hospital with multiple injuries…"

In the background several people were walking back and forth and I couldn't help but notice a young woman in a pink tracksuit walk behind the reporter twice, stopping both times to look into the camera lens.

'Has she no respect,' I thought.

"In the early hours of the morning Michelle lost her life and the police and her family are urging anyone with any information, no matter how small, to come forward."

The news report flashed to show an image of Michelle on a night out with her friends and I nearly choked on my custard slice.

"You OK Rox?" Brandon patted her on the back.

I certainly wasn't because the woman walking back and forth behind the reporter in the pink tracksuit was Michelle, dead Michelle.

"Crap," I said thinking quick.

"What's the matter?"

"I totally forgot I said I would go to Jennifer's tonight and help her with her science homework."

"Hey no probs I was gonna head home pretty soon I have gym again tomorrow and I haven't washed my kit."

"You don't mind?"

"Of course not."

After Brandon had left I went to my bedroom where Granda was looking at some of her posters on the wall.

"I need your help," I said.

"Sure honey."

"There's a girl been knocked over."

"Michelle?"

"Yes how did you know?"

"You left that page open for me to read."

I glanced down and sure enough there was a picture of the poor girl staring back up at me

"Oh, well I was just watching the news report and she's hanging around down by the place she was hit."

"We have to go to her," he replied concerned.

"Yes, but I'm going to need you to keep popping out to nana's to let me know if mum has set off. It's too late for me to be out and I don't want her to be mad."

"OK."

He disappeared and returned a few seconds later.

"She's still there and your nana was just dishing up cake so we have time."

"Let's go."

Lady Luck was definitely smiling down on us and we only had five minutes to wait for the bus that took us to the Beach Ballroom. I stepped off and made the short walk over to the crime scene. The area where Michelle had been hit was still cornered off with police tape and an officer was standing nearby. I scanned the area for Michelle and was relieved to see the poor ghost standing a little further down the road. We approached her cautiously.

"Michelle?" I said gently.

The girl quickly swivelled around to see who had spoken. She appeared to be in her early twenties and as well as a pink velour tracksuit she was wearing pink tennis trainers. Her hair was lush and quite long, and she had applied her make-up quite heavily, especially around her eyes.

"You can see me?"

"Yes."

"I think I'm dead."

"I'm afraid you are."

"My poor mum she'll be devastated, I'm an only child. I mean she was so disappointed I failed Beauty College but she was coming round, you know."

"I'm sorry," I said softly.

"Who are you?"

"I'm Roxanne McDonald and this is my Granda, Finlay."

"Recently deceased," Granda added.

"You're a ghost too?"

"I am lass. My Roxy here has been helping ghosts."

"Really because I know who did this."

"You do?" I said surprised.

"Hell yeah, that son of a bitch, Terry."

"Who's Terry?"

"My no good ex, and he was driving his friend's car. We'd only been going out like two minutes when I noticed his stuff appearing in my flat. Before I knew where I was he's telling me what to wear, checking my phone an stuff. So I kicked his ass out. He was way too suffocating."

She took a breath and rearranged her hair.

"Do you know the registration of the car?" I asked.

"I do indeed because it's personalised."

"OK, good. Do you think that's why you're here Michelle to make sure he's caught?"

"Damn straight, he's been stalking me for three months and the police wouldn't do bugger all."

"We'll help you, don't worry, I just have to figure out how to do this."

"Just go and tell that police officer," Michelle said and started to march over to where he was patrolling.

"I can't do that."

"Why the hell not?"

"Calm down, because I wasn't here that's why."

"And?"

"So I don't want to look like a complete loony."

"Oh."

"We'll figure it out," Granda said reassuringly.

"Ok then," Michelle said, pouting slightly.

"Let's make a call from a phone box," I said suddenly. "We'll give the registration and the description of the driver. If they get the vehicle there will be enough evidence on it surely."

"It's leaving a lot to chance," Granda said.

"What else can I do?"

"I think it's a good plan," Michelle added. "I reported him heaps of times. He hid in a bush outside my flat for seven hours back in February! Another time he slashed my car tyres and…"

"Michelle we need to do this now, I'm not supposed to be out this late."

"Oh OK, sorry, my mum says I go on a bit. Was I going on a bit?"

"Just a little but its OK. Do you know where the nearest phone box is?"

We walked up towards the main road in the city centre and found a phone. I shakily dialled through to the local police station.

"Hello," a woman's voice answered.

"Yes I have some information regarding the accident at the Beach Ballroom."

"OK I'll just take a few details."

"No personal details I just need to give you the information."

"I need details of all witnesses, ma'am."

"Do you want the information or what?"

"Go ahead, " the operator replied stiffly.

Having got all the details from Michelle on the walk up, I relayed them to the operator; the car registration, a brief description of the driver as well as the colour of his jacket.

"Right lets head home. Granda check to see if mum is still at nana's. Michelle, do you want to come back with us?"

"Sure, what happens now?"

"Well hopefully once they get your ex-boyfriend you will pass over."

"Like on Derek Acorah,"

"Sort of, let's get back home."

Granda disappeared and returned to say mum and nana were watching a recorded corrie episode. We jumped in a taxi at the city centre rank and headed home.

Help my Granda is Haunting Me!

Carrie was sitting patiently on my bed when we returned and we filled her in about Michelle. Michelle didn't seem at all comfortable with Granda or Carrie and she insisted on just talking to me. Within ten minutes I had a headache because, to put it mildly, she just didn't shut up. One minute she was telling us how angry she was about being killed, the next minute she was telling us about her holiday in Spain. Carrie and Granda chatted on my bed leaving me with our newest addition.

"I have to get back to school now Granda, Michelle would you like to come with us?"

"You haunt a school?"

"Yes, it's complicated, would you like to come?"

"No way, I mean, thanks and all but I hated school when I was there and I want to see my mum and find out what's happening to my apartment. I think I'll spend a bit of time haunting Terry the little...."

"Keep popping in and let us know how you are?" I said.

"Oh right, thanks Roxanne."

She popped out and left the three of us stood looking at each other.

"She was...interesting," Carrie finally said.

"I hope she'll be OK?"

"She knows where we are if she needs us."

Chapter 17

I was so glad when Saturday rolled round because I was invited to watch Brandon play rugby. Admittedly rugby is not my thing but Brandon had asked me to go and I wanted to so I could see him in action. Mum came with me too so I wouldn't look like some loser sat by myself.

I was totally shocked at how many of the girls from school had showed up to support him, he hadn't been lying about the female attention. We sat near the back of the stands where no one could really see us. When Brandon appeared on the field there was a gaggle of girls cheering embarrassingly. Brandon kept his head down and the game began. OK I don't mind admitting that if Brandon hadn't been playing I would have been totally bored to tears in about five minutes but he was something else. He literally ploughed through his opponents with such speed you couldn't help but be in awe. No wonder talent scouts were after him. My heart swelled with pride because he was mine. With each goal he scored I wanted to leap out of my seat and shout,

"Go baby!"

Sat with three of her friends near the front of the pitch opposite us was Tiffany. She was really desperate. Did I feel bad about being the cause of their break-up, definitely not! This was the girl who at the start of school last year scared the living crap out of a poor first year by screeching at them because they had accidentally stood on her designer bag. The poor little girl, already scared about her first day had been reduced to tears much to Tiffany's amusement. Her and her friends had had a real laugh as I'd led the little girl away to comfort her. She was getting a dose of her own medicine as far as I was concerned.

Brandon's team won of course and all the players hugged each other like proper men on the pitch. As they made their way to the changing rooms Brandon passed the front of the small crowd where Tiffany tried to talk to him and get his attention. He didn't totally dismiss her but his response was short and then he was on his way.

We set off home and Brandon texted to say he would grab a shower then head to ours.

"He's a lovely boy Rox, he seems to be making you really happy," mum said as we drove home.

"He does mum."

"You're nana is dying to meet him."

"I'll bet you told her about his appetite and now she's itching to knock up some grub for him?"

"How did you know?" she said smiling.

"Nana loves to cook, Brandon loves to eat, they are going to get on like a house on fire."

Mum had picked up a roast lamb joint from the butchers and when we got home she set about preparing it while I studied, yes you guessed it, the Mr Ratchet case. I really wished I could get Brandon to help me. He was the smartest boy I knew and I was betting he would have picked up on what I was missing. I didn't know why I was even looking through the same stuff over and over again it was so frustrating. I suppose I was doing it just to kill time.

"Hi sweetie," said Granda as be popped into my bedroom.

"Hi Granda, where's Carrie?"

"Visiting relatives and your nana is having a snooze."

"You want to read the paper?"

"Aye, that'd be lovely. Shame I can't have a cup of tea with it. You know petal you really should give all the Mr Ratchet business a rest for a few days. You need to recharge your mind, maybe try to get some fresh material?"

"It's bugging me."

"You're a perfectionist Rox. Relax a bit."

"You're right. I'll pick it up again on Tuesday when I'm studying in the library with Brandon."

"Nice boy."

"I know Granda."

"He'd better treat you right my lass."

"I know Granda."

"Or I might have to do a bit of haunting see."

"Honestly Granda," I laughed and pulled out my reading book for some leisure time instead.

I practically leapt from my seat when I heard the front door bell. Granda said he would find Carrie and give us a little privacy and with a pop he was gone. I opened the front door to a very happy looking Brandon.

"I was hoping to God that smell was coming from here, is that roast lamb?"

"I'm beginning to think you're going out with me because of all the extra food."

"No, but it helps," he grinned.

"Hey!"

"Kidding, kidding. It was great seeing you at the game, what did you think, were you totally bored?"

"No, not at all, you were great. I'm surprised you saw us with your following of fans."

"I know, I've learnt to block it out or it seriously distracts me from my game."

"What was Tiffany saying?"

"She told me it was a good game and asked if I wanted to go for ice cream. I politely declined."

"Good," I said firmly. "Hopefully she'll get the message soon."

We made our way through to the living room to wait for tea and see how much of a huge lamb roast Brandon could eat all to himself.

When Tuesday eventually came round I was no more relaxed. I was itching to get back to the Mr Ratchet case but I knew once I started I would be even more frustrated. I had tried to put it to the back of my mind but it was always there in the forefront of my thoughts.

Things had gone well with Brandon over the weekend but apart from a peck on the cheek Brandon was true to his word and was letting things move at my pace. Trouble was I didn't know what my pace was, or more to the matter, how to quicken it. I wanted so desperately to experience my first proper kiss, I was just at a loss as to when and where. I was also worried about Michelle. We hadn't heard from her again. I watched the news and her ex-boyfriend had been arrested but we didn't know if she'd passed over or not.

Brandon and I made our way to the library at lunch because he wasn't able to make it after school for our extra studying. He sat next to me pretending to do some algebra work while Tiffany, whose idea of a quick lunch was a cigarette, sat at the opposite end of the library staring daggers at us. Since our little rendezvous she had left me alone but I had the distinct feeling that she was lying in wait ready to pounce.

I had laid some of the pictures and articles out on the table and I retrieved *Blood and Granite* to see if there was anything I'd missed. I picked up a couple of other local history book to see if there was anything in those that might be of use, a blueprint perhaps.

"Roxy, do you want to get pizza after?"

"Sure."

Then just as I was contemplating whether I fancied Hawaiian or a meat feast something hit me. I looked at the page in the book I had stopped at. It was Mr Ratchet's office after he had been found out. It showed a policeman going through the drawers looking for evidence. I had seen it many times. It was old and faded and in black and white and really eerie looking. I looked down at the table and saw another picture. This one had Mr Ratchet sat at his desk holding his headmaster plaque. It was taken in his office too. He was sat smiling smugly behind his desk and beside him was a roaring fire…FIRE. My heart stopped. He was sat next to a roaring fire and it clicked. I looked back to the picture in the book. Same office, no Mr Ratchet, no fire either. The whole fireplace was gone; it must have been boarded up. Why would a fireplace be boarded up unless it was covering something up? I suddenly felt sick. I felt bile rise in throat and I had to actually fight to stop myself passing out. He had killed her accidentally outside his office and then dragged her inside and she had never left. Poor Carrie, I just knew I was right. My heart was pounding in my chest. I had to act. I couldn't believe I had sat not two feet from the dead body of a young girl on many occasions when I'd visited the headmistress's office over the past three and a bit years.

'Where are Granda and Carrie?' I thought desperately. I had stupidly said I didn't need them because I had wanted to be alone with Brandon. I didn't even know if they'd come back to school or if they'd just wait for me back in my room.

Feeling closed in and clammy I shot up and out of the library and in to the cool corridor so I could gather my thoughts and decide exactly what to do. I lent up against a wall and enjoyed a slight breeze coming from a nearby open window.

"Roxy, what's up?"

Brandon had stepped out after me. I looked at him and realised I couldn't do this by myself. If I told the police the chances are they would laugh at me. In my heart I trusted Brandon, I just hoped my gut was right. I didn't really have many options, I needed to get into the headmistress's office and I needed to bash through a wall. Even if Grandà and Carrie had been here I would still need someone to help me do it.

"Roxy?" he repeated. "Is something wrong?"

"I need your help," I said bluntly.

"Sure."

"When I ask you, you are going to think I'm completely mental."

"Try me?" he smiled reassuringly.

I took a very deep breath. "On the day of my Granda's funeral he came back to visit me as a ghost. Since then I've been able to see dead people and I've been helping them to pass over. One of them is a little eleven-year-old girl who can't pass because she was murdered and her body was hidden in this school and now I think I know where."

"Where?"

"The headmistress's office. Behind a boarded up fireplace."

Brandon remained calm.

"Right so what do you need to do?"

"So you believe me?"

"Of course I do."

"Are you nuts? You believe that I can see dead people, just like that?"

"Can you?"

"Yes."

"Well I believe you and I'll help you."

I looked at him sceptically waiting for him to run screaming but he didn't, he just waited for me to continue.

"I need to knock the fireplace through. I'm going to need a tool good enough to bash it down and I'll probably need you to do it."

He thought for a moment.

"I think there is a sledgehammer in the basement. The handyman has a tool cupboard down there."

"The basement." I said nervously.

"Yes, what's up?"

"Well, as well as the ghost of the little girl, there's a part of the headmaster that murdered her roaming around too and that's where he killed himself."

"Well the entrance is just round the corner. I'll nip down and you can wait outside."

"What if you get hurt?"

"I won't, come on."

He took my hand.

"We really gonna do this, now?"

"If you want to."

"Yes, I can't bear the thought of her body being there, it makes me feel sick, but what about the headmistress."

"We'll get the sledgehammer then get near her office and set off the fire alarm."

"That's actually a really good plan."

"I'm not just a pretty face."

Chapter 18

He led me quickly down the corridor toward the back of the school where the basement was located. I waited nervously outside still astonished that Brandon believed me. There hadn't been a hint of doubt on his face. If I didn't know better I would've say that he had known already.

He seemed to be gone ages but it was probably not even three minutes and when he returned he was carrying the biggest sledgehammer I'd ever seen. He grinned broadly.

"Got it, let's go." We made our way back the way we came and stopped just outside the entrance to the library which was quite near the headmistress's office. We paused to make further plans but just as I was about to suggest places we could hide once we set off the alarm something caught my eye. Standing behind the glass doors of the library were about twenty students. They were all starring at us, their heads twitching violently from side to side. I then heard a shuffling sound coming from behind us. I turned to look and saw a further dozen or so possessed students coming up the corridor towards us. The library door opened and the people within began to spill out. As they moved slowly and in time with each other, I backed up into Brandon.

"Bugger," I said.

"What the hell is this?"

"We need to go now. They're possessed."

We turned to head the other way but more students were coming up the corridor towards us. As we watched, the classroom doors began to open and more twitching heads joined the fast forming, slow moving mob.

"We're boxed in," Brandon said. "What do we do?"

"We need a loud noise. We need to break his hold on them," I said remembering that the first time in the bathroom my screaming and the deafening noise of the bin hitting the mirror had stopped Jennifer and Annabel.

Without hesitating Brandon gripped the sledgehammer with both hands. He brought it over his shoulder and then down with all his force onto a nearby window. The loud smashing noise echoed down the corridors and I brought my hands quickly up to shield myself from the glass shards. It worked and the first six or seven rows of people on all sides dropped, they stopped twitching and as they hit the floor I observed that several of them had nose bleeds.

"Do another quick!" I shouted.

He obliged with a little more pleasure on his face than I thought was necessary. Thankfully the corridor was blessed with lovely large windows. One by one Brandon smashed them until the whole corridor was filled with slumbering, passed out students and a few teachers too.

"We have to be quick," I said. "They will start to wake up soon."

We ran to the main entrance. On one side was the secretary's office and reception, and on the other was the headmistress's office.

"Crap," Brandon said.

"What...?"

My voice trailed off as the secretary stepped through the door all twitchy and possessed with no windows nearby to smash either. Brandon thrust the sledgehammer at me then ran at the poor woman and with an almighty rugby tackle knocked her to the floor. She was out cold.

"Was that really necessary?" I asked, smiling a little.

"Worked didn't it?"

"I suppose."

"Let's pop our heads round the door, Mrs Abbott might not even be in there."

Brandon tiptoed to the headmistress's office door opened it a fraction and peered inside.

"I can't see anything."

He opened the door and we stepped inside. Mrs Abbott had redecorated her office when she became headmistress ten years previous. The walls were plain beige and the furnishings where soft and welcoming. Her large polished mahogany desk was blissfully vacant. I breathed a sigh of relief and stepped inside.

"Roxy?" Brandon said apprehensively.

"What?"

"What's that on the floor next to the desk?"

I looked down. Two feet clad in Clarke's finest heels where sticking out the side of the desk.

"Crap and bugger it," I said. "Do you think she's passed…?"

I didn't get to finish. Quicker than a human possibly could, Mrs Abbott leapt from the floor onto the desk and was crouched down staring evilly at the two of us. Unlike the other possessed individuals I had seen, her eyes were not rolled back into her head. Instead the whole of her eye was as black as coal and her teeth were all sharp and pointed.

"Stupid meddling children," her voice was low and sounded like it had been slowed down. "Have you come to play with Mr Ratchet?"

Before either of us could respond Mrs Abbott jumped off the desk and punched me in the jaw. I'd never been punched before. You see people being hit on the TV and they brush it off like it's nothing. It was actually like being hit by a brick. She sent me flying back and I smacked up against the wall and landed in a heap on the floor. I winced and looked up to see she now had hold of Brandon by the front of his school shirt and she had him pinned on the back of the door. She used her spare fist to punch him in the face but he barely flinched.

"You can't have her, she is mine…MINE!" she screeched.

"Not for long you sick freak," Brandon shouted and with a bellow of pure rage he brought both his feet up and kicked Mrs Abbott in the chest. She fell to the floor and Brandon was on her in an instant, he flipped her over onto her chest, brought her arm up behind her back and pinned her to the floor.

"Quick Roxy, I don't know how long I can hold her."

"OK just be careful she's nearly a pensioner."

"Does she look close to retiring?"

Mrs Abbott was screaming and shouting obscenities I was pretty sure she had never uttered before. Brandon was buckling and struggling to hold her down.

"Maybe not, but she's gonna go back to normal hopefully so just try not to break anything."

I struggled to my feet. My back was sore, and my jaw was throbbing madly. With great effort I retrieved the sledgehammer and made my way to the wall were I was pretty sure the fireplace had been.

"NOOOOOOOOOOO!"

I ignored the mad screaming possessed lady and swung the hammer into the wall. It loosened some plaster and made a small crack.

"Bring it above your head babes," Brandon shouted encouragingly.

I ignored my achy bits and followed his instructions. I lifted the hammer up over my head, like I'd seen Brandon do earlier, and then with all my might I brought it down as hard as I could. This time the hammer embedded itself in the wall. I pulled and tugged and a large piece of plasterboard came with it.

"Keep going Rox, you're doing great."

I repeated the process over and over again. The hole in the wall got larger and larger; Mrs Abbott's screams got louder and louder. When the hole was big enough I gripped the edge and yanked a huge chunk of wall away. At the same time Mrs Abbott broke free and backhanded Brandon sending him flying over to the other side of the room behind the desk. In the blink of an eye she appeared in front of me gripped a handful of the front of my uniform and literally threw me against the door. I groaned as I landed badly on my wrist.

"Now you die Roxanne McDonald."

Mrs Abbott picked up the sledgehammer and began walking towards me. I tried desperately to get up but I was winded and I felt terribly dizzy. Her hair had broken free of its bun and was now wild, her eyes were as black as the night sky, blazing with evil. She looked wickedly down at her weapon.

"Just like old times." And then she laughed. I managed to crawl a little but her feet were just a couple of inches away from my face.

"Come out to play little one." I looked up to see her wielding the hammer with strength of a man rather than a thin woman in her fifties. I closed my eyes and braced myself.

"Keep your filthy mitts off my granddaughter Ratchet."

I thought I would cry with relief as I heard Granda's voice in the air and then a pop as he appeared beside Mrs Abbot. Seconds later Carrie appeared too and she immediately jumped inside Mrs Abbott's body. The headmistress began shaking violently.

"I won't give you up Carrieeeeeeeeee." The last word faded, ebbed away and Mrs Abbott dropped to the floor leaving Carrie stood there in her place.

"Look," Granda said pointing to the fireplace.

Sticking out of the hole I had made was a piece of fabric. The fabric matched the dress Carrie was wearing. I brought my hand up to my mouth.

"You found me," Carrie whispered in disbelief.

I struggled to my feet using a nearby hat-stand to aide me.

"Yes, I noticed the fireplace in one picture, then in another later picture it was gone. I asked Brandon for help...Brandon!"

Suddenly remembering I hobbled as quickly as I could round to him using bits of furniture to lean on. He was out cold but still breathing.

"It's happening," Carrie said suddenly.

I watched as the tips of Carrie's fingers lit up brightly. Granda ran over and they embraced.

"I'll miss you poppet," he said softly as the light spread up Carrie's arms.

"You too Granda and thank you both, thank you so much."

The light travelled up to her head until she was entirely engulfed by it. The light then started to cave in on itself until Granda was stood alone. I noticed a small tear roll down his cheek.

"Oh Granda."

"I know Roxy, she's gone to a better place but I can't help thinking I'll be lonely now."

"You have me Granda."

He smiled and I wished more than anything that I could give him a hug. A loud groan came from Mrs Abbott and I realised I had some serious fast thinking to do. I ran over and knelt down at her side just as her eyes flickered open.

"Roxanne, what are you doing here, what happened?"

"I'm not sure, I came to your office to show you something I had discovered, something important. You believed me and well…" I indicated over to the large gaping hole in the wall with Carrie's dress peeking out.

"What is that?"

"While studying I found out that the old headmaster Mr Ratchet had boarded up the fireplace in the short time he was here and there was one undiscovered body. I suspected that the missing girl had been put into the fireplace. Well I told you and you were mortified and insisted that we discover the truth. Brandon was with me so together we made the hole then that's all I remember. Don't you remember anything Miss? I mean you were pretty magnificent; you even had a go with the sledgehammer."

"It sounds familiar but my head is so fuzzy."

"I'll check on Brandon then I'll call the police. Just lie there a moment OK?"

Mrs Abbott nodded and I made my way back over to Brandon who had also started to come round.

"Roxanne. Why am I in the headmistress's office?" He said groggily.

My heart sank, please don't let him have forgotten everything.

"What do you remember?" I asked

"Last I can recall we were in the library studying."

"Really?" I thought I could actually cry.

"Yes."

I couldn't believe it, he had accepted my secret so well and it had felt like a major relief to have someone else know and believe I wasn't a lunatic. Sighing I recounted the same story to him that I had given Mrs Abbott.

"No way, you're telling me there's a little girl's body in that hole?"

"Yes and I need to phone the police. You just rest here; don't try to move if you feel dizzy."

Chapter 19

A massive investigation was conducted over two weeks following the incident. The police were baffled because the whole situation made no sense. Nearly the entire school was found unconscious or semi unconscious along the corridors outside the office, all the windows were smashed, a body of a young girl had been discovered in a boarded up fireplace and yet no one could remember a thing. I gave vague details mirroring everyone else's so I didn't stand out. The only person who seemed to remember anything at all was Mrs Abbot who vaguely recalled that she herself had knocked down the wall, discovering the lost body of Carrie. The police and fire brigade talked about chemical leaks.

Mrs Abbott was hailed as a hero and the remainder of Carrie's family where overjoyed to be able to finally lay her to rest. The entire school was shut for two weeks for various tests, to repair all the damage and so the police could close the murder investigation.

I was checked over by the doctor and luckily my wrist was just badly sprained. Nana insisted on coming in and staying for the whole fortnight to look after me but I didn't mind. It was lovely seeing Granda sat beside nana once more even if she wasn't aware he was there. Brandon came over most days and hung out. Nana fell in love with him in about two seconds and was whipping up a batch of homemade pancakes tall enough to climb. She loved to feed people and when Brandon tasted her homemade Cullen Skink he finished three bowlfuls then asked if he could take what was left home. He had an absolutely wonderful effect on my beloved nana and for the first time since Granda died I saw a big genuine smile on her face.

I finally believed in us. I relaxed totally within myself and when he left me in the evening I knew he would return. It was easy being with him, we talked for hours about everything and nothing at all and several times I was on the verge of telling him what had really happened that day at school. I only hoped when I finally plucked up the courage to reveal my secret, for the second time, that he would take it as well as he had the first time round.

We found ourselves led side by side on my living room carpet on Sunday evening, the day before we were due to go back to school and six days before the ball. Mum was taking nana home but not before she had baked a tray of Millionaire Short Bread which Brandon was slowly devouring piece by piece.

"So have you got a dress for the dance?" He lifted a piece of my hair and tucked it behind my ear. I shuddered slightly as his warm fingertips grazed my cheek.

"No, I'm not even sure they will still hold it."

"Sure they will it's a huge event. They will have a riot on their hands if they cancel it."

"I'll get one this week."

"You want me to come with you?"

"You want to come looking at dress's with me?"

"Well, no, but I would if you wanted me to."

I chuckled.

"Na, I'll get my girls to come with me."

"Cool, you want to order a pizza?"

"Are you for real? After nana's roast beef dinner barely three hours ago."

"I'm hungry."

"You're always eating. Is that your secret Bran, you're a binge eater. Newsflash, you are going to be fat when your metabolism slows down you know."

"Will you still like me then?"

"Of course although I'd rather you avoid it if you can."

"I'll do my best." He grinned, lent up against me to get his mobile out of his jeans' pocket and to my surprise ordered a huge pizza and garlic bread too.

As we walked to school the next day, Jennifer and Annabel told me they were planning on going to the dance together. When they suggested that we made it a threesome I decided it was finally time to tell them about me and Brandon. I was sure I could trust them to keep it quiet till after the dance but I was soooooo nervous.

"I sort of already got asked to go."

"Oh my God you mean like a date?" Jennifer gushed.

"Who is it?" Annabel said smiling.

"Well…erm…"

"Come on, come on, come on," Jennifer said. "Tell us already."

"It's Brandon."

Silence.

"Say something you guys."

"Are you two like official?" Jennifer finally said.

"Ish. I didn't want to shout it from the rooftops because Tiffany gives me a hard enough time as it is."

"How long?" Annabel asked.

"Only a few weeks."

"Weeks!"

I noticed Annabel's face drop but Jennifer was so happy I couldn't help but smile.

"I can't believe you kept this from us."

"I know, I wanted to tell you guys I just wasn't sure I believed it myself to be honest."

"And?" Jennifer squealed.

"And what?"

"How far have you gone?"

"We haven't, that's the thing. I said I wanted to take things at my own pace, which was great until I realised I don't actually have one."

"So how do you know you're even going out?" Annabel added with a hint of frostiness.

"He asked me," I answered defensively not at all liking her tone.

"OK so you've been going out for like, three whole weeks and you haven't kissed. Why the hell would he stay if you aren't putting out eh?"

"Annabel!" Jennifer exclaimed.

"Oh come on, don't tell me that her keeping this a secret doesn't bother you."

"Of course it doesn't and if I didn't know better I'd say you were jealous."

"Jealous, why would I be jealous of her going out with someone who goes out with anyone or anything with a pulse?"

"Annabel what's got into you?" I asked, trying to keep my cool.

Without answering Annabel stopped and headed in the opposite direction leaving the two us stood wondering what the hell had happened.

"Was it me or was that blown completely out of proportion?" I asked in disbelief.

"I've never seen her act like that. Do you think she fancied him?"

"Well we all sort of fancied him. Maybe I should have said sooner?"

"Ignore her she'll realise how stupid she acted and she'll come round."

"I hope so."

English and geography were first on the agenda but there was no sign of Annabel anywhere. The three of us never fell out so Jennifer and I didn't quite know what to do. We ate lunch together and avoided talking about it. Jennifer seemed happy just to hear every single little detail of my budding relationship and I was happy to tell her everything. By the time we headed for maths Jennifer was planning our wedding and saying what fabulous children we were going to make. Annabel had a different class for maths so we didn't know if she was bunking off the whole day. Mr Winters was sat at his desk when we walked in and he gave me a friendly smile which I returned. Brandon sat in his seat behind me to my left and I gave him a sly little wink as I sat down. Jennifer, not one for subtlety gave him an exaggerated wink leaving him with a puzzled expression.

I have never been so unfocused in maths before. Was this why I'd always got really good grades because I had no boyfriend to distract me. It didn't help that Jennifer had the biggest stupidest grin on her face the whole time.

"Jennifer you seem overly happy this morning. I had no idea maths was so exciting," Mr Winters said to her after a particular cheesy Cheshire grin.

"Sorry sir."

"Just let's do our work please." He didn't say it sternly but everyone in Mr Winters' classes had really warmed to him and he achieved something which very few teachers had, he had gained the respect of teenagers. The guy deserved an OBE. When class was over Jennifer and I waited outside. Brandon was the last out having stopped behind to discuss something with Mr Winters.

"Hey Brandon," Jennifer smiled.

"OK either you know or you are just plain weird Jen."

"I know," she grinned even wider.

"I think she's happier than I am," I said shaking my head.

"I'm just so happy that she is with someone."

"So are you girls going shopping for dresses?"

"Indeed we are," Jennifer said.

"Yes we are gonna catch late night shopping on Thursday."

"Well I am trusting you, Jennifer, to make sure Rox gets a lavish dress, I have big, big plans."

"What do you mean?" I asked nervously.

"Now that would be telling wouldn't it." He gave us both a cheeky smile and walked away.

"Oh my God, it's true, it's actually true; you two are going out."

"Doh, did you think I was making it up?"

"Of course not, it's just hearing him say it."

"I can't quite believe it myself sometimes."

"Roxanne," Jennifer asked calmly. "Please tell me how you are managing to keep your hands off him."

"Fear, pure fear."

We were now heading out of school and on our way home.

"Fear. What do you mean?"

"Look at him Jen. Look at him. And me."

"One day you are going to look in the mirror and realise you are gorgeous. I mean it Rox."

"I'm not stupid Jen. I'm a geek. Prettier than the average geek but still a geek, and I like being a geek. I like maths and I don't want to give any of me up."

"And you shouldn't have to. Has he said something to you?"

"No not at all. He's nice, sooooooo nice but…I dunno you see what type he usually goes for and…"

"What?"

"Never mind"

"Tell me."

"What if once we kiss I'm a disappointment?"

"You won't babes, trust me. Once you've had geek you never go back."

Chapter 20

When I got back home I checked Facebook to see if there was any word from Annabel. Nothing. It really made me feel sad, I couldn't remember ever having crossed words with her and it really hurt that she could ignore me like that. Granda walked through the wall at the side of my bed and saw me looking down.

"What's wrong pet?"

 "I fell out with one of my best friends."

"I know I was at school today. I hope you don't mind."

"No I don't expect you to float around all day by yourself."

"When another ghost comes on the scene maybe I'll have company."

"I know, maybe you could have a look for Michelle, I'm worried about her and there's never been anything about her case on the telly."

"I know I've been down the beach a few times but there's no sign of her."

"She'll swing by soon, if she hasn't already passed over."

"Probably aye, and by the way your friend is a little jealous."

"You think?"

Granda sat down beside me on the bed.

"Absolutely but she will come round and if she doesn't then she isn't as good a friend as you thought she was OK!"

"Thanks Granda."

"No problem. Could you flick the paper for me then, I'm going to spend the night with your nana."

I was a little concerned about Granda. With Carrie he'd had a constant companion and I could rest easy knowing he was never alone. Now she had passed over I worried about him being lonely. I needed to keep my eye out for stray ghosts on the street, maybe some sort of sign or advert in the paper could help.

Mum came home from work and I made us pizza; well I bunged a pizza in the oven. I watched telly with her and then I decided to do the maths homework we'd been given. I'd just sat down when my mobile started ringing in my pocket. It was Annabel.

"Hello" I said reluctantly.

"Erm, hi."

Silence.

"What's up Annabel?"

"I'm sorry OK!"

"You sound really sorry."

"Look I was totally out of order I admit it. It was just a shock and a surprise."

"I'm really sorry I didn't tell you sooner OK. When he first asked me I was sure it was some kind of joke and I didn't want to look like a fool."

"I'm sorry I didn't give you the support you needed."

"Friends?"

"Sure."

I smiled with relief and then we were chatting like nothing had ever happened, all was right with the world. We got onto the subject of dresses.

"I'm thinking of splashing out," I gushed.

"You have to. You need to show Tiffany Matthews that us lower plebeians scrub up goooooooood."

I laughed.

"You guys have to help me, we were thinking late-night shopping on Thursday?"

"Abso-bloody-lutly. Listen this is your mobile I'm calling and mum will kill me if she finds out so I'll see you tomorrow."

"Sure, we OK?"

"Of course Rox, you're my best friend."

Shortly after eight that evening our front buzzer chimed and my heart skipped a beat as I heard Brandon's voice crackle over the intercom when mum went to answer it. She let him in and he was up the three flights of stairs in no time. He wandered into my bedroom.

"Hey," he smiled.

"Hey."

"I was in the neighbourhood and I thought I'd drop on by and ta da…I bought ice cream and doughnuts."

He held up a Sainsbury's bag and I could plainly see a tub of Ben and Jerry's finest. He had fine taste.

"Come in," I smiled. "Mum is it OK if me and Brandon stay in my room?"

"OK honey but leave the door open."

I rolled my eyes at mum's reply.

He made himself comfy on my bed while I went and grabbed bowls and spoons from the kitchen. I took a seat at my dressing table and propped my feet up on my bed next to Brandon's.

"Good lord what size shoe are you!"

"Eleven"

"Holy crap!"

I scooped some ice cream into my bowl and handed one to Brandon who declined the bowl and ate the ice cream straight from the tub. I was never surprised at his lack of manners when it came to food.

"I have trouble finding decent trainers."

"I'll   bet."

"So how did the girls react?"

"Lots of questions."

"Like?"

"How long and how f..." I stopped and put my hand over my mouth.

"Far we'd gone?" He smiled finishing my sentence for me.

"Yes, they were hugely disappointed."

"Hmmm and are you?"

192

"No, well maybe, I don't know really."

"I wanted things to move slowly for you."

"Thanks, I think?"

He put the tub on the floor and sat up on the edge of the bed. I watched in slow motion as he leaned over towards me.

'Oh my God he's going to kiss me' a voice screamed inside my head, 'I hope my breath tastes of Rocky Road ice cream and not pizza'.

He was so close now I could smell his aftershave. He was so beautiful, like a work of art. I closed my eyes ready at last to kiss him for the first time.

"Roxanne," mum bellowed. We both jumped and Brandon sat back onto the bed.

"Do you and Brandon want hot chocolate?"

"No thanks mum."

"I'll have hot chocolate," Brandon piped up.

"OK mum," I shouted back.

"I guess there's a time and place huh?" he whispered.

"I guess."

"There's no rush you know I'm not going anywhere."

Chapter 21

By the time Thursday arrived I was seriously beginning to regret telling my two closest friends about my budding, lack-of-kissing relationship with Brandon. Not an hour went by without questions and interrogation. They wanted to know every minute detail of every conversation that had taken place. Annabel showed no sign of her little streak of jealousy, worse, the two of them seemed to delight in making me feel embarrassed and uncomfortable. Still it was nice to be able to talk about it but we sounded so boring on paper. It was different when Brandon and I got together it made sense, it was easy.

After school finished we changed in the girl's toilet (with no need to worry about possession from any essences of any sort) and headed to Debenhams. I had three hundred pounds in my purse from mum and nana to get the perfect outfit and matching accessories.

Our Debenhams was fab and stretched over three floors. Ladies wear was on the second so that's where we headed. We made our way up the escalators and I stared, completely lost at the rows and rows of ball gowns, fancy, frilly and puffy dresses.

"OK Rox what colour were you thinking?" Jennifer asked.

"I haven't."

"That's OK, what about shape, style and length?"

"Erm dunno, dunno and erm dunno. Wait a minute? Since when have you two been fashion experts?"

"We aren't. We are here for moral support," Annabel said. "Well if you have no idea we'll just try on a bunch and see what suits you."

They weren't kidding. The two of them attacked the rails with a vengeance grabbing dresses of all colours, shapes, sizes and various degrees of puffiness. Two shop attendants looked on at them, torn between amusement and distain. Next I was dragged to a changing room and was forced to try on dress after dress after dress. I had never had the need to dress up so formally; I'd never even been a bridesmaid or been to a ball before. Nothing seemed to suit me though, one yellow one made me look like a half peeled banana.

"There's this one," Jennifer said. "It's one of those that puffs out at the hips, this could be nice."

"Hand it over Gok," I said through gritted teeth from behind the changing room curtain. God it was worse than horrible. I gasped when the next one she handed me made me look like I'd put on three stone, not good. Soon I was fed up, deflated and ready to call it a day when Jen, wonderful Jen thrust the final one through the changing room curtain.

"I picked this one up on a whim Rox; I'm sure about the colour."

I took it and my first thought was that Jen was right. The dress was a deep forest green, a colour I always steered clear of. It had a fitted strapless bust, pinched in a the waist with a full skirt to just below the knee, the material was smooth like silk and the bodice had small delicate glass beading sewn onto it. I stepped into it, zipped it up then glanced in the mirror. I knew instantly that this was the dress. It fitted like it was made for me and made me look womanly and curvy. It was perfect and the colour looked amazing against my pale skin. I stepped out of the changing booth with a huge grin on my face. I felt like a proper lady.

"Oh my God, Rox that's beautiful," Jennifer (aka Gok) said.

"Holy crap that's the one," said Gok's side kick.

I couldn't help but smile. I had found the perfect dress, the hard part was over.

"Great now we just need shoes, a shawl and a handbag to go with."

"I don't need shoes, I have shoes."

It was true, I'd bought two pairs over the holidays and I hadn't had chance to wear any.

"We'll see, well don't just stand there, come on get that dress off!"

Another hour later, laden with bags and an empty purse, I grabbed a taxi home. Mum and nana were watching Corrie in the living room anxious to see my purchases.

"Let's see the dress honey," mum said.

"No way, you can wait till Saturday it can be a surprise."

"I came all the way here for nothing?" nana asked.

"No, you came all the way here to see your favourite granddaughter."

"You're my only granddaughter."

"It's a good job I'm so well behaved isn't it?"

"Hmmmmm, I see you inherited your grandfather's cheek. Is Brandon collecting you for the ball?"

"Yes nana."

"Good, that's how it should be. Well I'll make sure I am here then to see you off. He seems like a lovely young man, more than can be said for some of the waifs and strays that courted your mother when she was your age."

"Mum!" mum exclaimed.

"Well it's true. Now your Granda he was a real man. As gentle a dad and Granda as you could ever want but in the bedroom...a tiger."

"I think I'm gonna hurl," I gasped.

"I think I'll join you," mum added.

"You two wouldn't be here if me and your Granda had never....."

"La la la la," I cupped my hands over both my ears and retreated to the bedroom were Granda was resting on the bed. I could hear mum and nana's laughter echoing down the hall.

"Hello Tiger," I said when the door was shut.

"I know it's nice to know she thinks of me like that. In her day your nana turned many a head, I was really lucky she chose me. You should have seen her legs in a pair of stockings…"

"Please end the conversation right there."

"It's horrible getting old you know. In your mind you're still the same as you were when you were twenty."

"It's still totally gross sorry."

"How was shopping?" he asked changing the subject with a smile.

"Tiring but I got everything I needed."

"You seem happy with Brandon."

"I am and I know when I pluck up the courage to tell him my little secret that he will believe me because he did before even though he doesn't remember."

"And he will tell you his secret."

"How did you know about that?"

"Carrie told me what it is?"

"She did! Well tell me."

"He has to tell you himself petal. It's not bad but like your secret there has to be a right time and it has to come from him."

"That's frustrating."

"I image it is," he grinned.

I barely saw Brandon the next day at school, he had another big rugby game coming up and some swimming competitions and the coaches were grabbing every second of his time. My stomach was full of butterflies because it was the day before the ball and it was all everyone was talking about. Tiffany even seemed in good spirits having found a new piece of arm candy. I managed to nab Brandon briefly at lunch and he told me he would come over that evening to see me after practice. His coach had even taken away his free study period (meant for extra maths tuition) and the pressure was really on for him.

When I got home there was a note from mum saying she was working late and that there were microwave meals in the fridge for me and for Brandon. I opened the fridge, and bless her she'd nipped to Marks & Spencer's and got us a small selection. I padded through to the bedroom to see if Granda was there; he wasn't. I figured he was probably at nana's. I enjoyed the peace and quiet of being on my own, made myself a cup of tea and decided to go on the computer and listen to some music on YouTube.

Brandon arrived just after six and devoured ham and mushroom tagliatelle and a whole garlic bread I'd put in the oven.

"Anything for afters?"

"Brandon!"

"Hey I've had swimming and rugby practices today as well as regular PE. Damn coach is gonna run me into the ground."

"Poor baby," I cooed.

"I know and thanks for understanding and not bitching how little you've seen of me this last week. Will you come to more of the games?"

"Sure," I answered loving that he liked having me there. "Next game I'll be front and centre to cheer you on."

"I like the sound of that."

I had a rummage around in the fridge to see what I could knock up for his dessert. I wasn't even fazed anymore by the amount of food he consumed. I grabbed a microwave sticky toffee pudding and loaded it with three scoops of chocolate ice cream.

"You mum does the best food shopping," he said with a full mouth.

Mum chose that moment to enter and she smiled warmly when she saw Brandon tucking into his pudding.

"It's lovely to see a man with a healthy appetite."

"Thanks Mrs Mac."

She patted him on the arm, shook her head and went to make herself a cup of tea. After Brandon had finished we retreated to my bedroom. On the way he retrieved his rucksack from the hall where he had dropped it.

"I have something for you."

"I don't want your dirty gym kit thanks."

"It's not that dirty, here I got you these, I hope you like them."

He reached inside and pulled out a bag from Finnies the Jewellers. My eyes widened in surprise as I took the gift bag from his outstretched hand. Inside were two Links of London boxes.

"Brandon!"

"It's to wear tomorrow. Jennifer told me the right colour but I swear that's all I know about your outfit."

The first smaller box contained a sweetie charm bracelet with a little green gummy bear charm on it. The bracelet was made up of dozens of silver hoops on a clear elastic band.

"It's beautiful."

"Open the other one."

The bigger box contained the matching sweetie necklace.

"This is too much, it must have cost you a fortune."

"I told you I was going to make this as special as possible for you."

"You weren't lying"

"So you'll wear them tomorrow."

"Of course, oh my God I can't believe it's tomorrow. Can I go show these to mum?"

"Sure I'm gonna get going I'm totally knackered and I want to be well rested for tomorrow."

"You don't have to go."

"I know but I'll see you tomorrow. I'll pick you up at seven OK?"

"OK, my nana will be here too."

"I can't wait," he grinned.

The best thing of all was his smile was genuine.

Chapter 22

The next evening, the evening of the ball, I sat looking at my reflection and I just couldn't believe what I saw. My mum had given me a light coating of make-up including subtle green eye shadow to match my dress. They still hadn't seen me in it, I was cruelly making them wait until the final minute. The girl in the mirror that looked back at me was beautiful and I was comfortable saying that to myself. I reached into my wardrobe and pulled out the dress (which was hanging up, sealed in its Debenhams bag), and slipped into it. I teamed it with Brandon's gifts and the shoes I had picked. I'd also bought a small black clutch purse and Green butterfly clips for my hair.

I plucked up the courage to venture through to the living room where nana, mum and Granda awaited the big reveal.

When mum saw me her eyes started to fill up.

"My little girl is all grown up."

"Mum could you please get this out of your system before Brandon gets her?"

"I can't believe how grown up you look Roxanne," nana added.

"Thanks nana."

"I wish your Granda could have seen you."

He had, in fact he was sat on the sofa next to nana. He smiled and winked at me.

"I think he has you know."

My phone bleep bleeped from the kitchen table.

"Ooooo it's Brandon." I answered before it went to answer machine. "Hiya you're not calling to ditch me are you?"

"Absolutely not. Are you ready to go?"

"Yup."

"Cool, meet outside your flat in two minutes. You can bring your mum and nana down too."

Puzzled but curious I quickly stuffed my purse, phone and lip gloss into my new clutch and told mum and nana to come with her downstairs.

We all traipsed downstairs and stared up and down the street for the unexpected; we weren't disappointed. The four of us gasped (Granda muttered 'bloody hell') as a long white hummer limo came up the street and parked outside where we were stood. A driver got out and nodded briefly.

"Oh my God," I squealed.

The driver opened the back door, Brandon stepped out and he literally took my breath away. He was wearing a black kilt, sporran, a crisp white shirt and proper Bonnie Prince Charlie jacket. His hair was just as messy as it always was but I couldn't imagine it any other way. He looked absolutely mouth-watering.

"Roxanne you look amazing," he looked at me and I knew with my heart and soul that he meant it. I also knew, right then and there that this was no longer a crush, I loved him with every fibre of my being.

"You too Brandon, wow, and a limo, the Hilton is what three streets away?"

"It matters not my fair maiden, your carriage awaits." He nodded and smiled at nana and mum.

"You look after my granddaughter young man."

"I certainly will Mrs McDonald."

"Well you'll have me to answer to. Nice legs by the way," she said with a smile.

"Nana!"

"Well you two go have a good time and don't be back too late," mum laughed.

"Thanks mum, bye nana."

"Bye honey, bye Brandon."

I breathed a huge sigh of relief when we were at last alone in the limo. There were Thornton's chocolates waiting for me and champagne.

"One glass only," he said. "Your mum and nana will kill me if I take you home drunk."

"Thanks for being so great back there."

"No problem. Shall we drive round the block a few times?"

"Well seeing as we'll be there in two minutes, yes."

"The jewellery suits you."

"It's beautiful."

"So are you."

We drove around the block and drank our champagne before we decided to head to the ball venue. The school had hired a huge ballroom at the Hilton Treetops and it seemed they had spared no expense. A live band was playing to an already full dance floor. The tables surrounding the dance floor were decorated with black and orange table cloths while the centre pieces were glass skulls with tea lights in. There were orange and black helium balloon displays littered around too which all tied in with the Halloween theme.

I saw the next part happen as if in slow motion. As we walked in, the person nearest to me looked at us in disbelief and turned to tell her girlfriends. One by one everyone turned to look as we made our way to an empty table.

"Are they together now?"

"Is that Roxanne McDonald?"

I could hear the exclamations even over the music.

We took a seat and I was positively beaming. I wasn't used to being the centre of attention and I usually hated it when I was but I felt so magical and beautiful that I wanted to stand on a table and shout out how happy I was. It took less than five minutes for everyone in the room to know Brandon and I were together. It was official.

"Is everyone still looking?" I whispered after a few more minutes.

"Errrrr, pretty much yes."

"How embarrassing," I lied.

"Let's go check out the buffet," Brandon said slipping his jacket off and hanging it on the back of his chair. I followed him to the wonderful hot buffet spread that had been laid out. Baked potatoes, macaroni cheese, stovies and oatcakes. There were also cold meat platters, salads, cheeses and a selection of desserts.

Brandon grabbed a plate, handed it to me then took one for himself and began pilling it high with stovies. I, ever the lady, selected some cold meat, salad and a baked potato. We returned to our seats and ate our food. Jennifer and Annabel came bounding along soon after and joined us.

"What an entrance!" Jennifer gushed.

"You look really beautiful Rox."

"Awwwww thanks you guys."

"You wanna dance?" Annabel asked.

The live band had taken a break and a DJ was playing. I broke into a huge grin as *A Good Night* by the Black Eyed Peas came on.

"Sure, you coming Brandon?"

"I'll catch up with some of my boys, you go ahead."

He stood, bent down and kissed me lightly on the cheek making me blush.

"I'll catch up with you for a slow dance later, I promise."

I blushed even harder. Jennifer jumped up, grabbed my hand, I grabbed Annabel's and we made our way to the dance floor already bopping to the infectious beat of the music.

We hadn't quite made it on when Tiffany stepped out in front of us. I groaned. Something had to come along and ruin my perfect evening. Well I wasn't going to let a jumped up little cow like Tiffany Matthews ruin my ball.

"Tiffany just leave it," Jennifer said trying to diffuse a situation before it started.

"Leave it!" Her face contorted into anger "The queen of geeks steals my boyfriend and you tell me to leave it. You are sooooooo pathetic Roxanne. PATHETIC."

She made a lunge for me and in one fluid motion I shot the palm of my out and hit her flat in the stomach. The force shot her back, so hard in fact that she skidded backwards over the dance floor on her bottom and she came to a stop in the middle. I stared at my hand in disbelief. This was the second time that my strength had surprised the hell out of me.

With a scream so loud it could be heard over the music Tiffany shot up back on her feet and started running at me full pelt. I braced myself ready to fight, I wasn't backing down.

She was about three feet from me, arms out, when Mr Winters appeared, grabbed her arm and yanked her away.

"I think it time you were leaving Miss Matthews," he said calmly.

For a moment she looked as if she were going to plant one on our maths teacher. Then she seemed to remember where she was and looked utterly defeated. Her hair was squint and her lipstick had smudged. I didn't gloat, it

Help my Granda is Haunting Me!

wasn't my style but inwardly I was feeling pretty damn good. I watched with quiet satisfaction as she was led away by Mr Winters who turned and gave me a wink as he dragged her off. With the commotion over I sagged into Jennifer with relief, and her and Annabel gave me a warm group hug.

Then Brandon was there beside me, taking me in his arms and holding me.

"I only went to the bathroom what went on?"

We briefly explained and he was suitably furious.

"I'm not letting you go for the rest of the evening."

"That's fine with me."

As if on cue *Beautiful Girl* came blasting over the dance floor. Brandon smiled and led me gracefully to the dance floor. I was shaking like a leaf because everyone had seen the Tiffany commotion and now they were watching to see if I'd make a fool of myself on the dance floor. I hoped to God they were wrong.

"You look like you're gonna pass out Rox."

"I'm OK, I'm planning on burying my face in your jacket to hide my embarrassment."

"We've nothing to be embarrassed about. Ignore Tiffany she's just bitter and jealous."

"I know."

"Come here."

He pulled me to him and snaked his arms around my back, I brought my arms up and locked them behind his neck. Even though there was a considerable height difference we somehow fitted together like two jigsaw pieces. We moved together more gracefully than I thought was possible, mainly because Brandon was so good at leading and he emitted calming pheromones, or so it seemed. I glanced around to see that everyone had lost interest in us and was happy to see Granda sat at one of the vacant tables looking so out of place in his slippers but it was wonderful to see him there looking so proud.

"You look beautiful, so beautiful Rox," Brandon said recapturing my attention and then his look was serious and I just knew he was going to kiss me as he bent his head down. Butterflies rose in my stomach but I tilted my head to encourage him.

Our lips touched for only the briefest second but I had never felt so alive. Something within me awakened and our kiss deepened in response. I could not believe how good a kiss felt. Brandon's lips were so soft and one of his hands gently cupped the back of my head,

He broke away and smiled down at me.

"You're flushed Rox."

"I'm fine, that was erm…wow."

"I know, amazing." He face was serious once more. "Are you happy?"

"Honestly, I don't think I've ever felt so happy in my whole life."

A blinding light interrupted us and I turned to look for its source. My face dropped as I found it.

"NOOOOOOOOO!" I screamed.

Granda had stood up and was looking down at his hands, which was where the bright light was coming from.

I ran over as fast as I could.

"No Granda, please," I sobbed. "No, I didn't mean it. I'm miserable."

"It's fine petal. It's fine. I love you and I'm so proud of you."

"Don't leave me Granda."

A few people had heard something over the music and had turned to see, Brandon grabbed me and brought me into a hug so it appeared we were embracing.

"Not here Rox."

I sobbed uncontrollably into his shirt. The light travelled from Granda's hands up his arms and legs, I sobbed even harder, it was like losing him all over again, really losing him.

"Don't be sad Roxanne. I love you." The last three words were a whisper.

The light engulfed him then began caving in on itself until he was gone.

Brandon led me quickly away and out into the hotel gardens. He must think me totally mad, I thought but I was grateful he had helped me save face.

"Thank you," I said when I had composed myself.

"They can come back you know," Brandon said softly leading me to a bench in the middle of the gardens.

"What?"

"Ghosts. Once they have passed they can still visit for brief periods."

"You can see them?"

"Yes."

"Why didn't you say?"

"I wanted to find the right time to tell you. When we got rid of Mr Ratchet…"

"You do remember!"

"I did but you were forced to tell me your secret and I wanted to give you the opportunity to tell me on your terms knowing that I would be OK with it. That and I didn't want you to think I was different because I was immune."

"Wow. So we are both…what mediums?"

"No. You're a seer."

"A seer?"

"A seer is someone who communicates and guides the dead. Soon you should be able to summon spirits from the other side as your power increases. I can see ghosts but I can't hear them."

"If you aren't a…seer like me, then what are you?"

"Do you remember me telling you I had a secret?"

"Yes," my voice was barely a whisper.

"I'm a fairy Roxanne."

Chapter 23

I stared in disbelief.

"Oh come on Brandon you play rugby," I laughed.

"Not that kind of fairy ya dope. A real one."

"What you mean with wings?"

"Yes."

"You don't have wings."

"I do they are hidden."

"They must be pretty small."

"I'll have you know my wings are quite big for someone my age. They are hidden by magic, like my ears."

He lifted his hair up on either side of his head and right before my eyes the tops of his ears became pointed. He smiled and I wouldn't have thought it possible but he looked even more beautiful.

"Wow. Can I see your wings?"

"You're not going to freak out on me?"

"Of course not."

"I knew you would ask. I'll get them out but I'll have to take my shirt off."

"Why?"

"Well because they are hidden by magic so I can blend in and if they come back when I'm clothed I'll rip my shirt and its one of my favourites."

He stood and I watched him undo the buttons on his shirt, I bit my lip as more of him was revealed to me than I'd ever seen before. I stared at him in awe. His stomach was flat with each muscle clearly defined and breathtaking. It now made sense why he looked so perfect, no human being could be so beautiful and masculine at the same time. I waited, expecting his wings to pop out of nowhere but they spread out and upwards from behind his legs and stopped well above his head, a bit like a bird's wings spreading for flight. His wings were magnificent and beautiful. They were also huge standing about two feet above his head and were wider than his arm span. They looked like butterfly wings, with each looking like it had two parts that slightly overlapped. The top part was the biggest, slightly pointed at the top and curved down to his waist. The lower part looked rounder and ended at his knee. They were bluey green and metallic in colour and opaque apart from veiny parts branching out, thicker at Brandon's back and spreading out getting thinner towards the edges.

"Say something Rox."

"You are magnificent Brandon."

He smiled and his mighty wings flapped in unison causing all the nearby trees to bellow.

"Seeing as your taking this so well…" Before my eyes his skin changed. It went from a healthy bronze tone and paled to a glittering faint turquoise to match his wings. He looked like some mythical god. His skin glistened in the moonlight.

"This can't be real," I whispered.

"But you do believe, you have already seen the impossible in yourself."

I could only manage to nod in response, I was taking everything in.

His wings folded down and disappeared behind him, and his skin turned back to a tanned colour. I was disappointed but tried not to show it, I could have stared at him all evening. He took a seat next to me on the bench and began to put his shirt back on, I pouted a little.

"Do you remember me telling you that it was easier if I had a girlfriend, that the attention I get isn't as bad when I'm attached?"

"Yes, to be honest it's been bugging the hell out of me."

"Well humans are drawn to Fairies like bees to honey."

"Ah."

That explained the uncontrollable attraction I had for him.

"If I'm attached then it eases the following I have. It isn't their fault you see."

"What so if you don't have a girlfriend then you get a group of girls harassing you," I squinted in disbelief.

"It's true! Honest." He held his hands up. "I told you I had to take a restraining order out, I wasn't lying."

"Really?"

"Yes. She practically lived in the car park of my apartment for a month."

"Do I know her?"

"That's not important," he said quickly. "But what is, is that you understand that you are special, I want to be with you because I really like you Roxanne and I have for some time."

"Wow, thank you. Thank you for telling me your secret, and thank you for making this evening so special even if I was saying goodbye to Granda."

"I've got so much more to tell you."

"Go on," I urged.

"Not here, do you want to go back to mine. I have food."

"Always with the food."

"Well now you know why," he laughed.

"It's a fairy thing?"

"Yup, flying uses up heaps of energy and the magic I use to hide my wings and skin colour burns more calories than I can eat."

"Wow, well it makes sense I suppose."

"Do you want to take the limo or..."

"Or?"

"We could fly."

"Fly as in you...carrying me?"

"Yes but don't look so scared I won't drop you."

"I'm not sure, maybe the limo."

He laughed again, stood up and this time he didn't remove his shirt. His mighty wings appeared with a whoosh, there was a shredding of material and hearty laugher in the air. His skin had turned back to its natural blue and he stood before me in all his glory. I couldn't resist him. He held out his hand and I took it, trusting him without question. Before I realised what was happening he had pulled me to my feet, brought me to him and captured my lips. It wasn't a dance floor kiss, this kiss was deep and magical. The air around us fizzed with electricity and I ran my hands along his glittering arms, up his shoulders and locked my arms around his neck.

I felt my feet leave the ground and his wings moving, whipping the air around us. When he broke away I looked to see we were hovering about four feet off the ground and he held on to me as if I were made of feathers.

"Wow," I gasped.

"You are amazing."

"I'm amazing? You're fairy kisses are messing with my head making me dizzy."

"That's not my fairy kisses. Any supes are immune to fairy pheromones."

"Huh?"

"You're a supe, a supernatural."

Before I could question further or protest he hugged me tightly to him and with two flaps of his wings we soared into the Aberdeen night sky. I locked my arms tightly around his neck and wrapped my legs around his hips. I could feel his wings banging against my legs as we climbed higher and I held on tighter still.

"I need to breathe Rox."

"Whoops sorry," I said easing my grip around his neck.

Both his arms wrapped tightly around me and I finally relaxed. I nestled my head into his chest and I heard his chest vibrate as he laughed. The wind was whipping my hair fiercely as we climbed vertically until the hotel below us looked like a little shoe box.

"You OK?"

"Yes," I gasped.

"Don't worry, I won't drop you."

His whole weight shifted and we were propelling forward. It was peacefully quiet except for the sound of the wind rushing beneath Brandon's wings and his heartbeat which I could hear through his rib cage as I clung to him. The ride was smooth and now and again when I found the courage to look below I saw we were moving at quite a speed. Not before long I could see Brandon's apartment building. He landed swiftly on the flat roof and his wings disappeared behind him.

"Come on." He headed for the door, his skin turning to its human colour as he walked.

Chapter 24

Of course Brandon had the penthouse to go with the roof terrace. His apartment inside was modern and surprising clean. The roof terrace door took us into the living room and dining area. It was sparsely but tastefully decorated with two deep black leather sofas, a glass coffee table with a couple of issues of *Kerrang* magazine on it and the biggest flat screen TV I had ever seen on the wall. The walls were painted magnolia and the wall were the TV was mounted was wallpapered with heavy black and white embossed flowers.

The room doubled up as a dining room and at the other end of it stood a large glass table with heavy black iron legs and matching chairs.

"It's so tidy," Roxanne exclaimed.

"Well Eric cleans everything except my room," he answered leading me into the kitchen.

"So your bedroom looks like the bedroom of a normal teenager?"

"It sure does. Stick the kettle on, I'm just gonna change my   shirt."

I giggled at the huge tear in the back then admired his lovely perfect back, yum. I got a grip and stuck the kettle on, I noticed a tub of instant chocolate and I popped a few heaped teaspoons in a couple of mugs.

I was surprised how well I was taking all this news. It was hard to believe that just a few weeks ago I had been blissfully unaware of ghosts and fairies. It made me wonder what else was out there. I was also relieved beyond belief that I would see my beloved Granda again.

I made a couple of hot chocolates and took them through to living room just as Brandon appeared from a hallway off the living room.

"OK, there's so much to tell I don't know where to start." He took his hot chocolate and invited me to sit next to him on one of the sofas.

"Why don't your mum and dad stay here?"

"My mum, Jaselle, well she's my stepmum actually."

"Where's your real mum?"

"She died when I was a baby."

"I'm really sorry."

"It's sad but I don't remember her. Well mum hates it here."

"What has she got against Aberdeen?"

"It's not Aberdeen she hates, its Earth."

"Earth!"

"Yes, this is what I mean there is so much to tell."

"You'd better start from the beginning, gimmie the basics." I shook my head in disbelief.

"OK well most supernaturals are from a different realm, called Azealia. It's not nearly as big as Earth but it's more beautiful and totally untouched by technology."

"Wow."

"Some supes can shift in and out at will from Azealia using stone circles while some are stuck there permanently."

"What do you mean by supes?"

"Fairies are the dominant species. Weres are a close second but they are pretty territorial and they hate fairies as much as we hate them. There are dozens of different races and species including Vampires."

"Vampires, cool!"

"Ye well don't go imagining Brad Pitt, there's nothing romantic about vampires. They are ruthless creatures able to bend your mind at will to get what they want. They don't kill as many humans now but they don't have to really, they can make you their helpless servant in a second and you are rendered incapable of your own thought."

"Oh my God. Are there a lot of them?"

"In Azealia, yes they can't reside here on earth like us. That's not all, there are four realms all together."

"Four!"

"Yes," he laughed. "Jhalom is a realm for the deceased, humans call it heaven."

"That's where Granda has gone."

"Yes, when they light up as they pass it means they have passed to Jhalom."

"And you said he can come back?"

"Yes, ghosts can come and go for short periods if they are summoned and as part seer you will be able to summon him as your powers grow and are nurtured."

"I'll miss him, I've kinda got used to him being around. It's a huge relief to know I'll see him again. So the other realms?"

"Well where there is a heaven there has to be a…"

"Hell?"

"Yes, Morsith is the Hell realm and it's guarded by Hades."

"Hades."

"Yes, which bring us to the last realm, The God realm, Althea."

"Gods?"

"Yes, don't look so shocked Rox."

"It's a lot to take in."

I sunk back into the couch.

"You OK?"

"Yes I think so. Wow. So I'm descended from a seer."

"Yes. There aren't a lot of true seers left in Azealia but they command everything to do with dead."

"I wonder who it was, my relative I mean."

"Well we could try researching you're family tree these things can skip several generations."

"I never knew my father though."

"Ah, well we could look up your mum's side."

"I wonder how I can summon Granda?"

"I'll ask my dad, see if he knows anyone that can advise you, maybe try to get a seers book to help you."

"Wow, that would be great. Wait so you must have seen the times when Granda and Carrie met me or followed me around."

"I did and I knew instantly what you were because only seers can hear ghosts the rest of the supes only see them. There was a little girl with brown hair for a while too."

"Amy, long story regarding her, so did you know Mr Ratchet was there?"

"No but I'd seen Carrie and waved at her a couple of times."

"Ah," I smiled. "She told me you were special."

"There's one other thing I have to tell you."
"Oh just one other thing," I smiled.

"Yes well I chose the Halloween dance to tell you because there are two days of the year when the bond between Azealia and earth is at its strongest and its possible for a human to visit and it should be super easy with you having seer blood. Halloween is one day and the other is in April, in Chinese culture it's known as the Ching Ming Festival."

"And you want to take me to Azealia?"

"Yes, I want you to meet my family."

"Really."

"Yes, why so surprised?"

"What if they don't like me?"

"They are gonna love you."

I'd seen Brandon's Father and step mother so I knew that they were every bit as gorgeous as Brandon. I was going to look positively grey stood next to them but it was wonderful he wanted me to meet his parents.

"I'm so nervous now, how do we do it."

"Well Halloween isn't till Wednesday. After school on Wednesday I'll take you."

"Just like that?"

"Yes, my dad says he has taken a couple of his human friends and there's actually heaps of stone circle ions in Aberdeen."

"Really?"

"Yes, I mean there's literally hundreds littered up and down the country and that's what they are for."

"Ah, oooo so Stonehenge?"

"Yes it is but only supes that can turn invisible can use it because it's monitored too much."

"Gotcha, so we find a stone circle and then?"

"We hold on tight and when I shift to Azealia you'll shift with me"

"Sounds simple."

"It shouldn't be difficult."

"OK I'll do it."

"Great do you wanna order Chinese?"

"Brandon, honestly."

"You'll have to get used to it, I usually eat six full meals a day."

"You look beautiful when you're flying."

Help my Granda is Haunting Me!

"And you looked petrified," he laughed.

Nicola Ormerod

Epilogue.

When I returned to school on Monday I got a fabulously warm reception. OK slight exaggeration, a few extra people smiled at me and complimented me on my dress from the ball. Tiffany of course was utterly horrid, but in all honesty I was so unbelievably happy that I really couldn't give a toss how evilly she looked at me. More wonderful was holding hands with Brandon as he walked me from class to class. It was all new to me and it was just great that Brandon seemed equally as happy as I. I just knew deep down we were going to go the distance. We trusted each other with our secrets and I knew, like he, that we would never betray them.

In the evening I made my way to Brandon's apartment and we waited on his roof terrace for dusk. We sat side by side sipping hot chocolate and holding hands.

"Where are we going?" I asked.

"I thought we might go to the lighthouse its beautiful there at night. You can hear the waves crashing on the rocks and it's really quiet, serene."

"Sounds lovely. It was nice today at school."

"What was?"

"Just being normal you know. It was nice to just be us."

"My dad visited last night."

225

"Oh yes."

"Yup, he's looking forward to meeting you and..."

"And?"

"He knows a seer who's agreed to see you and maybe start teaching you how to develop your skills."

"Wow, that's cool. Another thing to crap myself over."

"Will you quit worrying, my dad already likes you."

"And your mum?"

"Well she not like your mum Rox."

"What do you mean?"

"I mean she's never been mean to me or anything but she's not mum material. She comes over as really abrasive."

"You sure she isn't Tiffany's mum."

"You might have something there," he laughed. "Don't worry if she isn't all warm and fuzzy it's nothing personal."

"Why doesn't she like it here?"

"She won't say but whenever they have to visit for school and stuff she spends as little time as she can. Dad visits maybe once a month and I like to visit them when I can. It's great visiting Azealia because I don't have to concentrate on hiding everything."

"Is it a difficult thing to do, hide it I mean?"

"At first it is but after a while it becomes second nature. It's harder to maintain if I'm badly hurt but as long as I keep my energy levels up I'm good."

"I still find it very hard to believe that you're an actual living breathing fairy but it makes sense. I've been so drawn to you for a long time."

"And I told you it's nothing to do with me being a fairy, you're totally immune."

"Then what is then Mr Clever Clogs?"

"It's Mr Fate."

"Hmmmmm I like this Mr Fate, he's a smart guy."

When the sky was fully darkened Brandon removed his t-shirt and with a sigh of relief his wings unfolded and I watched in awe as he stretched and flapped then. His skin turned sparkly blue and he held his hand out, helping me up. He brought his lips to mine and kissed me softly, caressing my hair at the same time. I was walking on air, literally. In one motion he embraced me tightly and took off. I gasped and broke away from his lips to smile up at him warmly. His face was serious and his eyes were hooded with worry.

"I think I love you Roxy."

"Really, why the worried face?"

"In case you didn't say it back."

"I do love you Brandon with all my heart."

He hugged me even tighter and whisked me into the night sky.

Coming Soon

Book 2

Help my Boyfriend is a Fairy!

CPSIA information can be obtained at www.ICGtesting.com
Printed in the USA
BVOW011752100113

310322BV00001B/2/P